WHO WANTS TO KILL THE DARLING?

MEL BORTHWICK
The film's director, whose wife threw herself off a balcony after Darling spurned her?

SAM COCHRANE
The cameraman, who suspects that Darling caused his teenaged daughter's drug addiction— and death?

GILES EADY
The screenwriter, desperately in love with the beautiful Erika himself?

ERIKA VON FARR
The beautiful film star who can never stop acting?

HONORIA FARQUSON
Her devoted aunt, who would hate to see Erika marry the wrong man?

A DEATH
FOR A
DARLING

E. X. Giroux

BALLANTINE BOOKS • NEW YORK

Library of Congress Catalog Card Number: 85-1758

ISBN 0-345-33024-2

This edition published by arrangement with St. Martin's Press

Manufactured in the United States of America

First Ballantine Books Edition: May 1986

This book is for Terry Fidgeon,
my doctor and my friend

CHAPTER ONE

Robert Forsythe felt a deep contentment. It was his favorite hour, early evening, his favorite month, May, and he was in his favorite sanctuary, the library of his home in Sussex. It had been far too long, he was thinking, since he'd had time to drive from London and spend a weekend here.

He sat at his desk, his long fingers sorting fishing flies into two piles, one lot to return to the metal box, the other to take with him. Dropping the last one, this a particularly fine specimen of lilac and orange, he shoved back the chair and stepped to the long window overlooking a stretch of turf leading gently downward to the pond. Rays of sunset, as vividly colorful as the fishing flies, gleamed across the water and outlined the higher branches of the plane trees. Sunset . . . May . . . days stretching enticingly out before him, days to fill exactly as he wished. Inhaling hungrily, he drew in clean country air redolent with fresh-cut grass, blossoming fruit trees, and the sharper odor of lime recently spread around the roots of the lilac bushes.

Miss Sanderson had been on the right track as usual and Forsythe smiled as he remembered his reaction to her demand that they take a vacation. With no hesitation she'd pinpointed his feelings. "Robby, you're positively hostile to the idea of leaving this office. You take after your father and are turning into a workaholic."

Abigail Sanderson was an authority on his father. For a number of years, before Forsythe had inherited her, she'd been his father's secretary. The younger Forsythe told her, "A week, perhaps even two, yes. That I can see, but a month . . . Sandy, it's out of the question."

"Nonsense!" One capable hand made a wide circle of their chambers, encompassing not only Forsythe's office, but also the reception area, the cubicle where she held sway, the room shared by two juniors, and the cramped storage area piled nearly to the ceiling with boxes and file folders. "You're married to these chambers. Robby, how long is it since we returned to law practice?"

"Several years."

"And in those years we've had our shoulders to the wheel, our noses to the grindstone—"

"To say nothing of keeping our eyes on the ball."

Slowly and with dignity she rose, and bestowed on her employer a long, glacial look. "You have no intention of speaking seriously. I'm wasting my time."

"Now don't you get hostile. I simply dislike clichés. State your case."

"Very well. You're exhausted and so am I. The Dawes-Hinton trial drew out to improbable lengths—"

"We did get them off, Sandy."

"Don't interrupt. The point is" —she ticked off points on her fingers— "young Peters and Vincent are quite capable of handling the practice for a month. In case you have reservations Eugene Emory is willing to act as consultant—"

"So you've been after Gene too."

She sank back into the chair and Forsythe took a closer look at her. Gray hair framed a face composed and austere but there were dark smudges under her eyes and lines he'd never noticed before across the brow, around the mouth. "You are exhausted," he said. "You're also right. We both need a break. A month it is. Tell me, have you made plans?"

"For the first week, yes. Duty calls. My sister Teresa is enjoying yet another honeymoon and wants me to substitute for her annual visit to a friend in Norfolk. I'm not charmed with the idea but Honoria looks forward to seeing Teresa and apparently she's a lonely person so . . ." Miss Sanderson sighed. "After that I'll indulge myself. I may go to bed and read."

"Good Lord! Yet another honeymoon. What is Teresa's score to date? Is it five or six husbands?"

"I'm afraid I've lost track. But her business sense is still working. The latest bridegroom is not only ancient but owns a shipping company. Anyway, Teresa's conscience was bothering her and she made me promise to spend a few days with Honoria. She has a large house and is wretchedly poor—"

"Odd combination. If your Honoria is wretchedly poor, how does she maintain a large house?"

"With difficulty, no doubt. And she isn't *my* Honoria. She was a childhood friend of Teresa's and I hardly know her. I do remember her father, the colonel." Miss Sanderson smiled. "I always thought of him as an ogre."

"Ugly?"

"Not in appearance. In fact I suppose the colonel was handsome in a cold forbidding way but he was a tyrant. Kept poor Honoria virtually a prisoner, drove his only son away from home, and then died a year ago leaving the poor woman that house, two old retainers, and a starvation income. Odd . . ."

Forsythe raised his brows. "Do I scent a mystery?"

"No. It just seems strange that a man as money-conscious as the colonel should fritter away a substantial amount of lucre in the last years of his life. Teresa says she thinks the old devil did it for spite—simply to enjoy the idea of his daughter eking out the rest of her life in poverty."

"The colonel does sound like an ogre. Has Honoria no relatives to come to aid her?"

"None that I know of. Teresa would gladly help but she doesn't dare offer. Honoria is proud and pride may be the only thing she has left. But enough of me, Robby. I don't suppose you've had time to consider your holiday."

He closed the file on his desk, the final one on the Dawes-Hinton trial. "Scotland," he said firmly. "I'll ring up the MacDougal and then I'm off to trout streams and peat fires and long evenings by said fires."

"And long days wading about and doubtless falling into frigid water. Shivering and cleaning slimy fish. Not my idea of Heaven."

"But mine." He stretched luxuriously. "I'll have to drive to Sussex to pick up my fishing gear. The Meekses will be delighted to see me."

Miss Sanderson grinned. "Mrs. Meeks won't be delighted."

"Posh. She'd like nothing better than to stuff me with home cooking."

"Mrs. Meeks is compulsively neat, Robby. And I've seen you prepare to visit the MacDougal. Looks like the sky rains fishing gear. Bet you."

"You're on. I win, you buy a drink our first day back at work."

Sticking her hat on at a jaunty angle, she opened the door. Over her shoulder she called, "Seeing you'll be paying, make mine a double."

Forsythe withdrew his gaze from the pond. The sun had set and he turned to switch on a lamp. The ginger-colored

4

cat had taken over his chair and as he bent to dispossess it the door opened. On the threshold Mrs. Meeks stood with her hands planted on her hips. Never had a person been so misnamed. The housekeeper, her considerable jaw jutting, cast a disgusted look over the reels, cases, creels, and rubber boots littering the carpet. "I told you I could pack this . . . this stuff for you." She added, apparently as an afterthought, "sir."

"And I thought I told you much of the pleasure of a fishing trip is sorting over the gear."

Bending, she prodded a rubber boot. "I do believe dried mud has dropped all over the carpet."

"Hardly. They look as though you've put them through the washer. Was there something, Mrs. Meeks?"

She clapped a hand to her brow. "Clean forgot. Miss Sanderson for you on the telephone, sir." As she said the secretary's name a note of approval tinged her voice. Miss Sanderson would never be guilty of marring a fine Aubusson carpet with assorted trash.

She stood aside to allow him to enter the downstairs hall where the phone was located and then busied herself brushing imaginary dust from the bannister, all the better to hear her employer's every word. As he picked up the receiver he wondered, as he frequently did, why he'd never bothered to put extensions in. There was no chance for privacy with this one. In his ear Miss Sanderson's crisp voice asked, "Do I buy or do you?"

"I owe you a double, but surely you didn't call to settle a bet. Are you having a good time?"

"Scrumptious. And I'm issuing an invitation for you to join us."

"You and Honoria."

"And a batch of houseguests."

Forsythe had a mental picture of those houseguests. Spinsters, perhaps widows . . . Sandy bored to tears and looking for some diversion. This time she wasn't going to manipulate him. "Nice of you to think of me, but tomorrow in the wee hours I head north to the MacDougal and that trout stream."

There was a pause and then Miss Sanderson asked sweetly, "Did you tell the MacDougal exactly when you were going to arrive?"

"I don't know myself. I'll travel in a leisurely way, pausing to drink in the scenery and partake of hospitality at picturesque inns."

"So, you see, no problem. You can drive up here tomorrow, do try to arrive for lunch, spend the weekend, and bright and early on Monday continue your trip."

"What are you up to now?"

Miss Sanderson was evasive. "Come along and see." She added, "It's seldom I ask you for a favor."

"It's seldom you don't." He glanced over his shoulder. Mrs. Meeks was practically breathing down his neck. "This is important to you?"

"Yes, and it is to you too."

Sandy was speaking as guardedly as he was. Perhaps she had an audience too. "I am not carting along a wardrobe that will be useless to me fishing."

"No worry. Come as you are. This is strictly informal. And Robby, I have a surprise for you."

"What?"

"If I told you it wouldn't be a surprise. I can promise you'll never regret this weekend."

Exasperated at his own weakness, Forsythe rang off. The redoubtable Miss Sanderson had an uncanny habit of being right, but there are exceptions to every rule. As it turned out, this weekend was to prove the exception.

CHAPTER TWO

Forsythe made no effort to arrive at his destination for luncheon. The shadows were lengthening as he drove through the village of Bury-Sutton, stopped to ask directions from an elderly man walking a poodle, continued over a covered bridge, and turned into a winding road that followed the River Carey's capricious course. Finally he swung the Rover between gateposts, noted that the gates standing open needed repair, spotted a tumbledown gatehouse, and piloted the car up a gravel driveway that wound as much as the Carey. The grounds echoed the forlorn entrance to the estate, shaggy grass much in need of clipping and untrimmed plantings. Turning the last curve he was pleased to see that the manor house stood among neatly clipped lawns and well-tended flower beds. The house was Georgian, with clean lines and pleasant proportions. There seemed no evidence of neglect on its imposing facade, no broken tiles or peeling paint. But then, Forsythe remembered, the colonel or ogre had passed to his reward only a year ago.

He pulled the Rover to a halt before the portico, crawled

out, and stamped his foot. His left leg, injured years before in a hotly contested soccer game, had stiffened up. Limping, he rounded the car and opened the trunk. As he lifted out his pigskin case, a low and ominous rumble sounded directly behind him. Glancing around he found the source of the sound. The mastiff was the size of a calf and brindled lips pulled back tautly from ivory fangs. "Nice boy," he said soothingly, and looked around for aid.

At that moment the door flew open and Miss Sanderson trotted to the top of the steps. "You're late," she told him tartly.

"Never mind that." Forsythe kept his voice low and soothing. "Do something about this monster."

The mastiff growled deep in his throat, small eyes appearing to be sizing up Forsythe's throat.

"Dratted animal. Would you believe he treed the milkman this morning?"

"Yes," Forsythe said faintly. "Call him off."

"No use. He won't pay attention to me. Look harmless. I'll get Potter."

Forsythe stood motionless, not daring to move a muscle, and tried to look harmless. Time passed, it seemed to stretch out into hours, then rescue arrived in the person of an ancient man attired in a threadbare butler's suit. He tottered down the steps and said sharply, "That's enough Heathcliff. Around to the back where you belong." Potter might have been old but he had good lungs. Heathcliff cast one last hungry look at Forsythe, backed away, and then reluctantly obeyed.

Miss Sanderson, who had prudently stayed behind Potter, joined them. "That animal should be chained, Potter."

"This is his job, miss; he's a watchdog and a good one." Rheumy eyes peered up at Forsythe. "Sorry about that, sir. Heathcliff's bark is worse than his bite. Your case, sir."

"He didn't bark," Forsythe pointed out, and surrendered his case.

"Perhaps, miss, you could show Mr. Forsythe to the drawing room while I take his case up."

Miss Sanderson linked arms with her employer. "Don't look so surprised, Robby. Haven't you seen a butler before?"

"Not for a number of years and never one quite that old. White side whiskers!"

"He's one of the retainers I mentioned. The other one is his wife, an inspired cook. The Potters practically raised Honoria. Her mother died when she was born and the colonel wouldn't allow her to attend school. Honoria had a succession of governesses but the butler and cook looked after her." Miss Sanderson paused to catch her breath and then said indignantly, "And the ogre made no provision in his will for the Potters."

"You seem to have made good use of your time, Sandy. Soaked up the family history."

"More than I really wanted to. The colonel was a heartless brute." As they entered the house her voice changed. "Isn't this charming?"

The hallway was as gracious as the exterior. It was spacious, with gleaming parquet, a magnificent flight of stairs, and a vaulted ceiling. It was also bare, furnished only with a side table bearing a telephone and a china urn of lilacs. A uniformed maid appeared from a doorway to the left, bobbed her head, gave Forsythe a shy smile, and ducked into another room. "It doesn't look as though Honoria is suffering financially," Forsythe muttered. "The grounds around the house are practically manicured and—"

"Honoria does most of the gardening herself. She has a boy in from the village to cut grass and that's all. As for the maids . . . that's part of the surprise."

Miss Sanderson led the way down the hall, and as Forsythe followed, he wondered what the surprise was. Could Honoria have come into an inheritance? No, Sandy

9

had mentioned she had no living relatives. Miss Sanderson swung open one panel of a set of double doors and turned to give him a wide smile. Warily he approached, bracing himself for a gaggle of middle-aged women. There was only one middle-aged woman and she was hurrying to meet them with both hands outstretched.

"So pleased, Mr. Forsythe. Abigail thought you'd be here much earlier. Did you have difficulty locating the house?"

"None," he told her.

Miss Sanderson made introductions while Honoria Farquson beamed up at him. She was as tall as his secretary but much heavier. She'd be handsome, he decided, if she were wearing something besides that shapeless flowered dress, those heavy oxfords, and if she had that amazing hair properly styled. At first glance he had thought her hair white but now he could see it was that rare shade of blonde that glints silver. Honoria's skin was delicate and high-lighted with rose-pink. Taking his arm she led him toward the trio of men who had risen from around a low table.

"You must meet my guests," Honoria told him and proceeded to introduce him. Forsythe could see what Sandy had meant by informal. The men wore faded blue jeans, sweatshirts, and sandals. There any resemblance ceased. Samuel Cochrane was enormous, and reminded Forsythe a bit of the mastiff. With some trepidation he allowed his hand to be swallowed in a massive paw, but apparently this giant felt no need to emphasize his strength with a bone crusher. Cochrane merely gave him a firm but gentle squeeze and relinquished his grip. Beside Cochrane, Melvin Borthwick looked like a terrier, if a terrier could be pictured as totally bald. As though to make up for the hairless skull, Borthwick had shaggy brows and had cultivated an equally shaggy mustache. The youngest man was about Cochrane's height but he had a build that more resembled the greyhound lines of Sandy's figure. Funny, Forsythe thought, how his mind kept running along canine lines. Giles Eady, the greyhound, shook hands, gave a sudden and radiant smile that made his homely freckled face charming, and asked, "Did you by any chance make the acquaintance of Heathcliff?"

Forsythe smiled back. "I did; luckily the butler came to the rescue before he had a piece of me."

Waving them into chairs, Honoria said contritely, "I'm sorry Heathcliff startled you, Mr. Forsythe. I suppose he should be chained but actually he's a comfort in a place like this."

Giles transferred the charming smile to his hostess. "You may have to change his name. Mickey has a strong objection to it."

"That's a shame but Heathcliff had his name before Mr.—" Honoria clapped her hand over her mouth. Looking guiltily at Miss Sanderson, she murmured, "My tongue does run away with me. I nearly spoiled your surprise." Turning to her latest guest she told him, "We were hopeful you would arrive for luncheon but you are in time for tea. I've been holding off hoping the young people would be with us."

"Might as well forget about them," Borthwick, the terrier, told her.

"Right," Giles agreed. "Young lovers, you know, and a day in May."

Honoria nodded and reached for a bellpull. "I suppose so. We'll have tea but there's Marcia too. She should have her tea. I'd hoped to have all the guests gathered when you arrived, Mr. Forsythe, but the young people went to Bury-Sutton and Marcia is feeling miserable. A head cold, you know, all stuffed up and can't breathe properly and so I told her directly after luncheon, 'You simply must go up and rest.' The only cure for a cold is rest—" Breaking off, she glanced over Forsythe's shoulder.

11

"Relax, Honoria, Marcia is here," a vibrant voice announced.

Honoria bobbed to her feet. "Do you feel better, dear?"

"I feel like death warmed over. My head's pounding like a trip-hammer but I couldn't rest, just twisted around."

Wondering if this could be the surprise, Forsythe got to his feet and turned. This woman wasn't entering the drawing room; she was making an entrance. She'd paused, holding her tall body in the hipshot pose of a model. She was heavily and expertly made up, her dark brown hair expertly styled, a simple white suit of stunning elegance displaying every curve of a full and fine figure. She didn't wait for introductions but told him, "I'm Marcia Mather." Then she waited expectantly as if for applause.

Knowing some reaction was expected, Forsythe said, "Delighted, Miss Mather," and glanced at Miss Sanderson for enlightenment. The enlightenment came from Giles Eady. He hooted with laughter. "Don't look so puzzled, old man. Marcia's waiting for you to rave on about seeing everything she ever appeared in, assuring her you're a devoted fan."

"Don't be silly, Giles," Marcia said and finally moved, taking the chair Forsythe was holding for her. "One can't expect every person one meets to have seen one's films. Anyway—" bitterness tinged the vibrant voice— "I've never been a star, only a supporting actress."

Forsythe tried to make amends. "I'm sorry, Miss Mather. I know little about actors or films. I seldom attend the cinema."

"Except for one particular actress," Miss Sanderson said wickedly.

Forsythe shot a look at his secretary but Miss Sanderson was demurely watching Potter trot in, carrying in shaking hands a tray bearing a fine Georgian silver tea set. Everyone was watching the butler, collectively holding their breaths,

12

wondering if he would reach the table safely. He did and lowered the tray shakily in front of Honoria. As she busied herself with the teapot, she told Forsythe, "Marcia is an old friend—"

"*Old*. You make me feel like Methuselah."

"I didn't mean it that way. I meant we've been friends since nursery days although in later years we've seen little of each other. That's another reason I was so happy about this weekend." Forsythe watched Honoria extending a cup to Marcia. Those hands, so close together, summed up his impression of the two women. Marcia's hands were the texture of the white silk of her suit, the oval nails flawlessly painted the same color as her lips. Honoria's hands were well shaped but with roughened skin over the knuckles, the nails clipped short. A capable hand, Forsythe thought, strong and tranquil. He found he preferred the pleasant dowdiness of his hostess to the actress's lacquered dark beauty.

Leaning back, Marcia smiled, a smile of remembrance. "My father called us the Three Musketeers. Remember, Honoria?"

"Three?" Borthwick's bald head turned from Marcia to Miss Sanderson. "Are you the third?"

"My sister Teresa is the third musketeer. There was an age difference, five years between us. It makes little difference now but when you're children it means two separate worlds, two separate sets of friends."

Briefly, Forsythe wondered which way the age difference went, but Miss Sanderson wasn't about to volunteer the information. Sandy's age was her carefully guarded secret.

"We were inseparable," Marcia continued. "Marcy, the doctor's daughter, Terry, the vicar's child, and Honey, daughter of the lord of the manor."

"Hardly a lord," Honoria murmured.

"Well, he certainly acted the part," Marcia retorted with a touch of asperity.

13

"I don't suppose the colonel was too popular; he was such a forceful man. Odd." Honoria brushed back a straying gilt lock from her brow. "I always called him father but I think of him as the colonel."

"Or ogre," Miss Sanderson muttered to Forsythe.

Touching a minute hankie to the slightly pinkened tip of her shapely nose, Marcia turned her attention on Miss Sanderson. "And Teresa has married again? Which number is this one, Abigail?"

"I've rather lost track."

"Let me see." Oval nails ticked off fingertips. "The first one was Howard . . . I do remember him. Teresa married for love and Howard was young and good-looking and penniless. She never made the same mistake again. Her other husbands have been creaking with age, not much to look at, and wealthy—"

"Mustn't be catty, Marcia." A deep voice chimed in with the thud of a bass drum and Forsythe jumped. It was the first time he'd heard Cochrane speak and the man's voice matched his size.

"I'm not being catty. As a matter of fact, Sam, I happen to agree with Teresa. This love stuff is for the birds."

"You should be an expert on that," Giles told her.

Marcia swung on him. "Now who's being catty? As for you, Giles, it's the pot calling the kettle black!"

"Break it up, children," Borthwick said sharply. "We've enough problems without bickering."

"Problems is putting it mildly." Giles slumped in his chair, his freckled face suddenly morose. "Want to bet the first thing Mickey asks when he gets back is whether I've rewritten that scene he was whining about?"

Slamming her cup down on the table with unecessary force, Marcia told him. "He's got practically every line of dialogue now. And look at me. Five lines, for God's sake."

"You do tend to exaggerate," Giles told her.

"Well, six or seven." She turned an irate face on Borthwick. "You're supposed to be the director, Mel. Don't you have any control over that ass?"

Forsythe found he was sitting on the edge of his chair. "Pardon me, but is this a film company?"

In the shadow of the bristling brows Borthwick's tiny eyes glinted. "Part of one. Giles is the scriptwriter, as Marcia just made clear; I'm suppose to be the director, and—" he raised a hand. "No, Abigail, I'm not conspiring to keep this part a deep dark secret. Men must stick together, after all we're practically an endangered species."

Forsythe eyed Marcia. "And you've a role in it?"

"A cameo," Giles said.

The woman's painted lips curled. "A high-sounding term for a bit part. A few lines now and if Mickey has his way I'll be totally mute and with my back to the camera. *Cameo*."

Forsythe turned his attention to the huge man beside the director. Cochrane was slow spoken and slow moving and gave an initial impression of bovine placidity. His eyes gave lie to this. They were wide set, feverishly bright, and constantly in motion, flicking from one person to another, from one object to the next. "And you, Mr. Cochrane, you're an actor too?"

"Let's drop the misters. I'm Sam if you're Robert." Forsythe jerked his head in agreement and Cochrane continued, "I'm only a cameraman."

Borthwick gave a sharp bark of a laugh. "Modest old Sam. He happens to be the best cameraman in the British Isles. We're lucky to have him, Robert."

So . . . they were all on first-name basis, Forsythe thought. He didn't care much for the quick switch but when in Rome . . . Honoria was now offering homemade Madeira cake and talking in fast bursts. "You have no idea how excited I was when they chose my home for location, I think that's what it's called, for their film. A dream come true!

15

From the time I can remember I've been stagestruck, Mr. Forsythe. We have a literary club in Bury-Sutton and since the colonel's death I've had time to join in and appeared in a play." The charming rose-pink heightened in her cheeks and she confided, "Mr. Borthwick has offered me a part in this film. Oh, not exactly a part. An extra they call it. All I have to do is stand around with a group of people with a shopping bag over my arm and—"

"Very much like my role," Marcia muttered.

Forsythe noticed with amusement that Honoria Farquson hadn't yet succumbed to informality and was still using misters. "May I ask the name of the film?"

"No," Miss Sanderson said flatly.

"Come now, Abigail," Borthwick chided. "I can see no harm in that. We're doing a remake of *Wuthering Heights*."

"Brontë." Forsythe glanced around the drawing room. A pleasantly shabby room with much-faded chintz. "No doubt I'm displaying ignorance but I can't see this as a suitable setting."

"How right you are." Giles pushed his cake plate back and grimaced. "When we finish this thing, if we ever do, it will bear little resemblance to that epic. This is what is called a contemporary treatment of a classic. Everything up-to-date in Kansas City and even the title has been discarded." He winked at the director. "I suggested *Heathcliff Goes to the Dogs* to our Mickey and he says I'm not funny."

"I think you are." Marcia chuckled. "It's perfect. My God! Mickey seems to think the role of a brooding Heathcliff should be acted like a poor man's Marquis de Sade."

"I know," Borthwick agreed dourly. "This morning when he was running through some lines he kept twisting his face as though he had a nervous affliction."

"There's only one possible thing that can pull this one through." Cochrane's deep voice turned all heads in his

16

direction. Those restless eyes flickered over the articles on the tea tray and fastened on a point behind Forsythe's left shoulder. "Thank God Catherine—"

"Sam!" Miss Sanderson said sharply.

"Sorry, Abigail. Nearly let the cat out of the bag."

Forsythe had had enough. "I'm getting a bit tired of this talking in circles. Sandy, what is all of this about?"

"Patience, Robby, is a virtue." She glanced around. "Shall we change the subject?"

"Excellent idea," Marcia said. She patted a hair into place, examined her nails, and asked demurely, "That actress Abigail mentioned, the one you go to see—may I ask who she is?"

While Forsythe was trying to find a way of evading an answer, his secretary blurted, "Erika Von Farr. Robby's not only gone to see all her films but he's even seen some of them twice. Didn't you see that one . . . what was the name? Ah, yes, *Dark Decision*, at least three times, Robby?"

Forsythe could have twisted her neck. What was wrong with Sandy? Normally she was reticent not only about her own affairs but even more about his. This conversation made him feel foolish, having to confess to infatuation with an image on a screen. He mustered as much dignity as he could and said slowly, "I very much admire Miss Farr. She had tremendous talent, and yes, Sandy, I did see that film three times. I particularly liked the last scene."

"Moving, wasn't it?" Marcia smiled but it was only a jerk of the painted lips. "Let me see. Erika was mounting a staircase and her lover, who had betrayed her, was at the foot. He says something like 'Forgive me' and Erika says—" she deliberately flattened the vibrant voice— " 'Forgiveness is impossible but I promise I'll do my best to forget you.' "

This parody of his favorite scene sent blood into Forsythe's face. He felt they were laughing at him but the

17

other three men showed no signs of amusement. Giles Eady said cuttingly, "The words do seem trite, my little cat, but I agree with Robert. It wasn't the dialogue; it was Erika. Every line of her body showed grief and outrage, the way she stood, half-turned, her hair flung in a single fluid line down her back . . . no tears . . . dry eyes that made tears appear merciful—"

"Oh God! Do spare me, Giles." Marcia dabbed at the pinkened tip of her nose with a lacy scrap. "I'm sick as a dog and I can see not only you but Sam and Mel are ready to pounce on me as though I've defiled the Mona Lisa. I apologize. I agree Erika is a magnificent actress but—" malice crept into her voice— "it would appear not everyone is overwhelmed by her. Did you read that interview when Erika first arrived in England? It was written by a woman . . . Riverdell?"

"Roverdale," Cochrane corrected. "I read it. The writer was a witch."

"Truly a nasty woman," Honoria said indignantly. "I felt Miss Roverdale was consumed with envy."

"Nonetheless," Marcia said, "much of what she said was the truth. Erika *is* built like a boy. And that bit about her face . . ."

"Rather too much brow and too little chin," Giles said. "Knowing you I imagine you didn't bother reading the responses to Miss Roverdale's criticism." He sat forward, his hands knotted into fists. "One letter to the editor said that Miss Roverdale appears to equate udders like a cow and a pretty face with talent. The writer said there were quite enough curvaceous talentless actresses and too few with Erika Von Farr's genius."

"Another letter put the whole matter into a nutshell," Borthwick said.

Dreamily, Forsythe quoted, " 'Magic is not a matter of face nor form. Magic is the ability to convince one that an actress is beautiful without beauty, ugly without ugliness, young without youth, or old without age. Magic is a quality Erika Von Farr is blessed with and because of this we are all blessed."

"Bravo!" Marcia clapped her hands. "Keep this up, Robert, and you may join Honoria as an extra in this immortal film."

Forsythe was crimson with embarrassment. Not only that but he had finally, and it was past time, put all the threads and innuendoes together. He knew what Sandy's surprise was, he knew what they had been talking around, and he was stricken with panic. He felt as he had before stepping onto the stage in a school play. The tea and Madeira cake felt leaden in his stomach. Stage fright! The barrister who had dominated many court rooms had perspiration drenching his palms, knees that were shaking. Dimly he was aware that Sandy was regarding him with the indulgent concern of a mother about to watch her son eat too much rich dessert and become sick. Honoria and her distinguished guests were chatting and making rather too much of not looking at him.

Then Sandy stiffened, turning like a pointer toward the door—that damn dog simile again. Forsythe couldn't turn. He felt paralyzed. Please, he begged, don't let me make a fool of myself.

Then a voice resounded from the direction of the door. Forsythe paid no attention to the words, all he heard was the familiar voice that could vary in tones from the whisper of black satin to the silvery swish of a rapier blade.

The other men jumped to their feet. Slowly Forsythe pulled himself up and as slowly turned.

19

CHAPTER THREE

Erika Von Farr wasn't making an entrance. She simply strolled in and Forsythe avidly drank her in. He couldn't argue about Miss Roverdale's remarks. Erika did have the build of a boy: tight jeans strained over narrow hips, a loose sweatshirt displayed only a hint of curves, and her shoulders were wide and thin. Long hair was pulled back and held with a bit of yellow yarn and her face, which perhaps did have a bit too much brow and not quite enough chin, was dominated by huge, luminous eyes.

Forgetting completely about the other people he found himself irresistibly drawn to her. She extended a cool hand and he clasped it in both of his. He opened his mouth but before he could speak Marcia called from behind him, "What Robert's going to say, Erika dear, is that he's seen everything you've ever acted in and he's president of your English fan club."

"With the exception of being involved in a fan club, that is the truth," Forsythe confessed shamelessly. "This is an honor, Miss Farr."

"Erika, please, and it's my honor. I've heard so much about you."

Had Sandy been babbling on about him? Forsythe wondered. "I'm a barrister."

"And also a detective. The California papers picked up some of your cases—the one involving the sculptor, Sebastian Calvert, and that terrible one last year where the three school girls were murdered on the moors."

Forsythe found he was still clinging to her hand and released it. As he led her toward the tea table he assured her, "I'm not a detective, not in the actual sense of the word. I've more or less fallen into a few cases and been lucky." He tried to steer the young woman toward a chair beside his own but Giles was already holding a chair between his own and Honoria Farquson's.

"Wouldn't it be exciting if we were to have a nice juicy case for you to solve this weekend?" Marcia asked.

"Marcia, *really*," Honoria protested.

Reaching over, Marcia patted the other woman's hand. "Not blood and gore and bodies in the library, only something to demonstrate Robert's detective ability. Something mild . . . say the theft of a priceless diamond necklace."

"A thief in *my* house!"

Erika darted a look at the older actress and said with the swish of rapier steel in her voice, "This is Marcia's idea of a joke. Pay no attention to her, Aunt Honoria."

Forsythe looked from his hostess to the girl opposite him. "Aunt?"

"A carefully guarded secret," Marcia told him. "Apparently the only person Honoria confided in is Teresa and she's never breathed a word. Honoria, you might have told *me*."

"How could I, dear? I hadn't seen you since we were girls." Honoria turned placidly to Forsythe. "Yes, Erika is the only child of my brother. I'm terribly proud of her but to

21

talk about it would have seemed like . . . well, boasting. My brother died and Erika's mother took her to California. Erika was only about six weeks old at that time and we only met again recently. As a matter of fact that's how I met the rest of my guests. I was chatting on about this house and Mr. Borthwick said he'd like to see it because it sounded like the setting they needed in their film and . . . well, here we are.''

Miss Sanderson beamed at the barrister. "When I got down here and saw Erika I knew how surprised you would be to meet her, so—"

"You swore everyone to secrecy and lured me down here, Sandy.''

"Are you sorry you came?"

"No, certainly I'm not sorry." Forsythe wasn't. His eyes drank in Erika. For a bad moment before she'd arrived he wondered if the magic the actress projected in the shadow land of films would disappear in the real world. It hadn't. Her pale skin was as flawless now as it was before the cameras and wisely was not even touched with cosmetics. The lashes framing those luminous brown eyes were luxuriant and her every move had an unconscious and amazing grace.

He realized he was staring and wrenched his gaze from Erika. Potter was entering the drawing room, bearing fresh tea and another plate of thinly cut sandwiches. Giles was talking to Erika. "Where's the wonder boy? Lost him along the way?"

"A nice dream," Marcia muttered and accepted another cup of tea.

"Mickey decided to run back from the village," Erika said. "Felt he needed exercise, so I drove his car back."

Gile's charming smile flickered. "Wonders will never cease. Mickey allowed you to drive his precious Ferrari. Love is a wonderful thing.''

Honoria was glancing at her watch. "I do hope he gets back soon."

"He'll be a while yet," Borthwick told her. "Probably out in the garage wiping every speck of dust off that gleaming finish."

Everyone with the exception of Forsythe and Erika laughed. Rose-pink color, much like her aunt's, flooded into the girl's face and she said hotly, "You love making nasty remarks about Mickey, don't you? He enjoys quality goods and takes care of them. Would you prefer him to neglect his possessions?"

"Small chance." Borthwick was laughing. "Remember what happened to that little script girl who draped Mickey's leather jacket around her shoulders when we were on location in Spain? He had her fired on the spot."

"And what about that business when poor old Carruthers slipped into Mickey's dressing room and nipped a swallow out of his bottle of scotch? Pure murder!" Giles said.

"Stop it!" Erika was on her feet.

"Do sit down, dear," her aunt soothed. "I'm sure they're only joking."

Dividing a dark look between the director and the writer, Erika slid back into her chair. Forsythe tried to distract her. He asked, "Who is Mickey? Or is that a secret too?"

This time it was Cochrane who answered. "The famous Michael Dowling, known to multitudes of adoring females as Mickey Darling."

Erika was still irate. "Now you're doing it too, Sam. I expect this picking away from Mel and Giles, but you!"

The feverish eyes in the broad placid face flickered in the girl's direction. "It happens to be the truth, Erika."

"Oh, what's the use?" she muttered.

Marcia said brightly, "You must have seen our Mickey Darling, Robert. You said you'd seen all Erika's films and Mickey co-starred in her latest. What do you think of it?"

Forsythe was beginning to dislike Marcia Mather. Now she'd turned her malice toward him and was doing it gleefully. He *had* seen the film she'd mentioned and had been terribly disappointed. There had been a few moments when Erika had managed to inject life into it but mainly it had been dull and even vaguely funny. There had been rather too much of Dowling's profile and bare manly chest and he seemed to have most of the dialogue. The problem was, the man, despite his amazing good looks, was absolutely wooden. As Forsythe tried to think of something tactful to say he was saved by Giles Eady. The writer was echoing one of his thoughts. "If it had been billed as a comedy it might have gone over," Giles said lazily.

"It was drama and you damn well know it," Erika said. "Mickey didn't have quite enough experience at that time. He hadn't ripened as an actor."

"I thought he was a bit overripe," Giles retorted.

Erika was on her feet again. "I'm not sitting here and listening to this another minute. It's unfair to Mickey and—"

"What's unfair to Mickey?"

The man they'd been discussing stepped over the low sill of one of the long windows leading to the garden. Michael Dowling, even in a loose exercise suit, was as handsome as he was on the screen. Drops of perspiration dotted his bronzed brow but every hair on his curly head was in place. The famous profile was presented to Forsythe, and when Honoria hastily made introductions it barely moved. Dowling lifted a negligent hand. "Hi, Robert. Now who's been taking my name in vain?" Without waiting for an answer he took a chair beside Honoria and bent forward to see the writer. "While I was dusting the Ferrari down I thought—"

His words were drowned out in a gale of laughter. Even Honoria was trying to turn a chuckle into a cough and Forsythe felt the corners of his own mouth twitching.

Dowling looked puzzled and Erika told him, "Pay no attention to these oafs, darling. What were you going to say?"

"I was going to ask Giles if he'd rewritten that scene."

"As a matter of fact I didn't. Thought we'd better discuss it."

"Nothing to discuss. I gave you the notes I made on changes."

Giles wriggled around on his chair, pulling a rumpled batch of papers out of a pocket in the tight jeans. "I think you'd better reconsider. Mel and I kicked it around and if we do it your way we're going to lose the effectiveness—"

"What's wrong with my ideas?"

"In the original script Heathcliff chases Catherine down a winding road on his motorbike. She's running and every motion shows she's terrified, like a mouse with a cat on her heels. Sams says that will be good from the camera angles, very dramatic."

"So? I didn't put any changes in there."

"The changes start as soon as Heathcliff wheels the bike in front of her, narrowly missing her, and then jumps off, looming over her. In the original script Heathcliff simply looks down at her—"

"Through the face visor of a helmet. I told you when I get off that bike I take the thing off. You can't see my face and what people come to see is Michael Dowling, not a damned helmet."

"Keep your shirt on and let me explain. The outlines of your face through the plastic visor are glimpsed. This way gives an ominous, mysterious look to Heathcliff. Anyway, you leave on the helmet, pick Catherine up like a doll, and throw her on the back of the bike. Then you roar away and the camera—you tell him, Sam."

Cochrane's restless eyes moved toward the writer and then returned to their scrutiny of the sandwich plate. "It

25

would be a dandy shot. Catherine's profile outlined against that brutish helmet, her hair blowing over the lower part of her face . . . picture it, Mickey."

"I have and I don't like it. I want to take off that damned thing and—"

"And make a speech you've jotted down here," Giles snapped. "It sounds like a soliloquy. Along the same lines as Friends, Romans, countrymen . . . It doesn't read, Mickey. Heathcliff would never talk like that."

"This Heathcliff does and that's the way it's going to be."

Giles and Dowling were glaring at each other like two turkey cocks and Forsythe was wondering dismally how Emily Brontë would have reacted to Heathcliff roaring around on a motorbike chasing Catherine doubtlessly attired in blue jeans. He jerked his attention back to the two men and found that Borthwick was trying to act as peacemaker. "Be sensible, Mickey. Giles and Sam and I agree the scene should stay as written. Erika, speak up and say what you think."

"I think," she said placidly, "an actor has a sense of role and it's up to him to decide how he wants to act it."

Marcia examined her nails and muttered, "Love is *really* blind."

The famous Dowling profile swung on her. "You keep your trap shut! Mel, I could care less what you and Sam and Giles think. Erika agrees with me and we're the artists. Rewrite it, Giles."

"And if I won't?"

Forsythe waited for an explosion but Dowling merely touched the handsome column of his neck. "I need a drink."

"I've rung for fresh tea," Honoria told him. "Ah, here Potter is now."

Dowling waved the tea aside and told the butler, "Never mind that. I'll have a scotch and soda."

26

"There is no scotch, sir."

"I had scotch last night, Potter."

"You, ah, finished the bottle, sir. Would you care for brandy?"

"*No.*"

Honoria's face flooded with color. "I'm so sorry, Mr. Dowling. I had no idea. I'd send down to the village but I'm afraid everything is closed now."

The handsome mouth appeared to be setting in a pout and Honoria looked on the verge of tears. It was Giles who told her gently, "Not to worry. If Mickey wants scotch he can get it from his room. He always has a good supply of Glenlivet. As a matter of fact I could use a drink." He winked at the director. "What about you, Mel, and Sam? Better bring down the bottle, Mickey."

"I'll settle for tea," Dowling said hastily. He prodded a sandwich. "What is this? Watercress? I loathe watercress."

Honoria turned the plate around. "There's fish paste on this side. You like that."

He scooped up a handful of dainty sandwiches and turned his attention on Giles again. "As for you, genius, if you don't want to do it my way you can get the hell out. No two-bit hack—"

"Giles happens to be the best scriptwriter in London," Borthwick told him crisply.

"I couldn't care less. Dozens of writers would jump at the chance of working with me." As an afterthought he added, "And Erika. Shape up or ship out, Giles."

Pulling his greyhound body from his chair, Giles glared down at the actor. His expression was murderous but he kept his voice mild. "Nothing would give me greater pleasure. Having my name on the credit list of this dog would be embarrassing. Get yourself another hack."

"Both of you cool off," Borthwick ordered. "You do have contracts."

"Contracts are made to be broken," Dowling said, around a mouthful of sandwich.

"I want Giles and I *do* happen to be the director. You stay, Giles."

The writer's mouth snapped open and Erika reached up and touched his arm. "Please. For me, Giles."

He looked down at her and Forsythe caught a glimpse of his expression. The naked emotion in Giles's face told the whole story. His shoulders slumped and he said, "Mel?"

Borthwick flung his hands up. "Rewrite it Mickey's way."

"Peace at any price, eh? Okay, I'll get started."

As the writer ambled toward the door Borthwick pulled his terrier body up and jerked a thumb at Cochrane. "Should have time before dinner to check the lighting in that upper hallway, Sam."

Honoria, murmuring something about dinner preparations, left close on their heels, and Erika, after dropping a kiss on Mickey's cheek, followed. Marcia made no move to leave and lit a cigarette, staring moodily at the spiral of gray smoke drifting up from it. Dowling had apparently forgotten the unpleasantness and was demolishing a thick slice of cake. For the first time since being introduced he acknowledged the barrister's presence. "Hear you're another one in love with Erika."

Forsythe stiffened but it was Miss Sanderson who said coldly, "I told you Robby is a fan of hers, not—"

"Same difference. Marvelous girl, of course, and she makes an adequate Catherine. Whole movie hinges around Heathcliff, though, and I'm having a devilish time seeing that role gets full exposure. Everyone fighting me—even Sam."

If he was waiting for Forsythe to commiserate with him he was to be disappointed. "I know nothing about film-making," Forsythe told him curtly. He was thinking of that word—adequate. *What* a term to use to describe Erika Von

Farr. He changed the subject. "How did this house come to be selected for the film?"

"Erika's aunt came up to meet her in London. Funny, Erika's over thirty now and it's the first time she ever met her aunt. Of course, this is also the first time Erika's been in England. Did most of her work in Hollywood and some on the Continent but never England. Erika introduced her aunt around and auntie started dithering on about her house. Mel was sorry for the old girl—it was pretty plain she was broke so he offered to rent the place for the movie." Dowling added generously, "I had no objection. Kind of keeps it all in the family."

"You and Erika are to be married?" Forsythe asked faintly.

"As soon as auntie gives her blessings. If she doesn't I'll talk Erika around and we'll get married anyway, but in some ways Erika's pretty old-fashioned and her aunt is her only living relative." He eyed the last piece of cake and then lifted it onto his plate.

Forsythe was wondering how to break away. Neither Marcia nor Miss Sanderson seemed inclined to make conversation, so the barrister finally asked, "You're an American?"

"Sure am, Robert."

"God!" Marcia grunted and got to her feet. "I'm not sitting through another rerun of 'Yankee Doodle Dandy.'"

"Better watch that mouth or what went for Giles goes for you too," Dowling told her.

"I happen to have a contract too."

"Your part *can* be rewritten."

She shrugged an elegant silk shoulder. "So what? You have me down to about six lines now." She bent and butted her cigarette. "A word of advice for old time's sake, Mickey. If I were you I'd be padding my role, not paring it."

"Is that a threat?"

"Let me put it this way. We're overdue for a nice long chat."

"We've nothing to talk about."

"That's where you're mistaken. And don't leave it too long. Coming, Abigail?"

Miss Sanderson paused only long enough to pat Forsythe's shoulder. "See you at dinner, Robby."

Forsythe looked longingly after the two women, wondering how to break away from Dowling. He had no chance. Dowling was unleashing a flood of words that sounded rehearsed, and in a short time the barrister knew what Marcia meant when she'd said "rerun."

"Yes," Dowling drawled as though nothing had intervened, "I'm an American, a true-blue son of Uncle Sam. Born and bred on a small farm in the Midwest . . ." Forsythe heard all about Dowling's early life and then perked his ears up. "—and I admit women have always helped me along the way. Never men. Take my chance to get off that godforsaken farm. I was seventeen and just about going nuts and then one of my high school teachers came to my rescue. Miss Pike had a face like her name but the fluttering heart of a girl. She put up the dough for me to go to Los Angeles. Said she was interested in my mind." Here Dowling closed one eye in an exaggerated wink and leered suggestively at the older man. "What Miss Pike expected was for me to send for her and she would 'share my life.' Fat chance!"

Forsythe was no longer bored. He was repelled. Hoping to wind up the confidences, he said hastily, "And I suppose when you got to Hollywood fame and fortune were waiting."

"No. A string of menial jobs was waiting. I did some of everything—working in fast food places, pumping gas, parking cars. Then another woman came along. This time it was Junie, who turned out to be an agent. Not one of the topflight ones but she was not doing badly. I parked her car for her and a couple of days later she moved me into her apartment. Said she was interested in my talent." Here Dowling went through the same wink and leer again and Forsythe fought off the impulse to drive his fist into that leer. "After Junie and I played house for a couple of weeks I got restless and told her to find me movie work or I was spreading my wings and flying out of her life. She managed to get me a few bit roles. It wasn't great but it was better than pumping gas or parking cars."

"Bit roles?"

"Parts where I only appeared once. For instance, in one monster movie I was the guy that pointed at the giant praying mantis about to devour a town and yelled, 'Hey, look!' That sort of crap. It was a drag but that was the way I met Marcia Mather. Her name doesn't carry much weight now but at that time Marcia was recognized as a damn good supporting actress. The movie she was appearing in was one of those beach sagas and Junie had got me a part as a lifeguard. Marcia was supposed to come wandering along the beach, spot me, and stop to see if I'd seen so-and-so. The old girl took one look at yours truly in bikini trunks and that was it. Must admit she didn't beat around the bush. Didn't pretend she was interested in talent or mind, just what Mickey had stuffed in those trunks."

Dowling paused and for a bad moment Forsythe thought they were going to go through the wink and leer routine. But the younger man was fishing out a gold cigarette case and matching lighter. He selected a cigarette, made no move to offer his companion one, and lit it. "So . . . Marcia and I set up housekeeping. Just about broke Junie's heart but what the hell. Marcia could do more for me than Junie. But Marcia had no intention of helping me; she just wanted to keep me on a leash like a poodle. I soon set her

31

straight. Either she'd use her clout to get me a decent part or it was bye bye doggie. Once she got the idea she did her best but couldn't come up with a thing. I had a couple of screen tests . . ." Dowling turned an astounded look on the barrister. "Would you believe the damn fools said I couldn't act my way out of a paper bag?"

Forsythe believed it devoutly but mercifully he was spared answering. Dowling rushed on. "I started getting restless and Marcia was at her wit's end. God, but she was infatuated! Jealous as hell. If I looked at another woman she went into a tantrum. I tightened the screws and then she had an idea. She'd always wanted a starring role so she figured she'd fix me up and herself too. She had a fair amount of money stashed away and she borrowed the rest and we produced our own movie. A romantic version of the Trojan Wars—"

"A contemporary treatment?" Forsythe asked, thinking of Emily Brontë and *Wuthering Heights*.

"No, a period piece. Togas and the whole business. I liked the idea. Look great in togas." The actor paused again, this time apparently to savor the picture of his magnificent body displayed in a toga. Then he sighed. "The movie turned out to be a disaster. I was Paris and Marcia was Helen. The reviewers cut the poor old girl to pieces. As one of them said, 'Marcia Mather as the immortal Helen couldn't possibly have launched a thousand ships. Mather would be lucky to launch a leaky canoe.' From that time on her career went steadily downhill while mine went up. I took the lead in a string of oaters." Dowling grinned at the barrister's perplexed expression. "Westerns. I look almost as good in cowboy clothes as I do in a toga and the girls went wild. Screamed and sobbed and tried to rip my clothes off for souvenirs. Fan clubs started and I was away."

"What about Miss Mather?"

"Had to leave her behind. From then on she would've

32

been dead weight. Know it sounds cold but that's survival. I steered clear of Marcia and the first time I've been near her since is on this movie. Mel's a softhearted guy and he gave her a bit part because he felt sorry for her. Then we found out she was a childhood friend of Erika's auntie and I got stuck with her this weekend. All Marcia's done is make snide remarks."

Forsythe pondered. Did Dowling have any idea or did he care what kind of impression he'd just made? He'd exposed himself as the most selfish, unfeeling man Forsythe could remember meeting, and there he sat, looking complacent. "I suppose Erika Von Farr was the next woman to help you with your career."

"Didn't meet her right away. Had to struggle on by myself for a while, Robby—"

"My name is Robert," Forsythe said icily.

At his tone the actor looked up, examined the barrister's long head, light brown hair, and wandered down the elegant length clothed in well-cut tweeds. "Abigail calls you Robby."

"Miss Sanderson is the only one who does."

"Don't get huffy. What's in a name? I get Mickey Darling all the time and I'm not crazy about it, but it is good business. Anyway, after I starred with Erika I became hot property. From now on they're going to pay through their noses for the services of Mickey Darling." He glared at the silver teapot. "God, I wish I had a drink."

"Why didn't you take Giles's suggestion and bring down your Glenlivet?"

"And have those freeloaders gulp it down? I make a practice of not sharing booze. If I started offering drinks around they'd bankrupt me. Hey, Robert, what do you think of this house?"

Startled by the abrupt change of subject, Forsythe

33

glanced around the drawing room. "I haven't seen much of it but it seems charming."

"Charming and imposing but I got a hunch it's a white elephant. Going to be tough to unload. Have to spend a fortune modernizing this place. It needs central heating and decent bathrooms and the hot water supply is crazy. Either comes boiling out of the tap or it's ice cold. And, Robert, believe it or not, there's only one telephone in the whole house. Out in the hall. Can't even have a private conversation. In my house in Hollywood there's a phone in every room, even in the bathrooms. What do you think of that?"

Not much, Forsythe thought. Aloud he said, "Sounds most convenient. Are you and Erika thinking of living here with Miss Farquson?"

Dowling flung back his head to laugh, exposing the bronze column of his throat. "Not this Yankee Doodle Dandy. No, our headquarters will be in Hollywood. Erika has some damn fool notion of keeping this place on, but that's just sentiment. The old family home and that sort of rot." He cast a dissatisfied look around the comfortable room. "We'll have to unload it and that's going to be tough."

"Perhaps the house would be difficult but the land is valuable."

Dowling's head swung around. "The land . . . what do you mean?"

Silently, Forsythe cursed his rash statement but it was too late. "Did you notice the housing estates on the other side of Bury-Sutton?"

"Housing estates? Oh, you mean subdivisions. Hey, I see what you mean. There's good money in that business. Lots of land around this house too. Wonder how many acres auntie has."

Forsythe again felt a sense of revulsion at the avarice in Dowling's expression and voice. Just what had he started?

He pointed out, "I hardly think you need concern yourself. Miss Farquson is not old and she obviously loves this estate."

"Auntie will be better off in a smaller place. And so will those two servants. That butler can hardly creep around, although I must admit his wife is a great cook." Pulling his long frame up, he walked around the room. He paused by a superb piecrust table and drummed his knuckles against it. "Know anything about antiques, Robert?"

"Very little," Forsythe said hastily and untruthfully.

"Thought you would, you being English."

"Being English is scarcely synonymous with being an expert on antiques."

"Abigail was saying you have a country home yourself. Been in the family for centuries and full of old stuff." Plucking up a Dresden shepherdess from the mantel, he spun it around. "You must know something about values. What about things like this?"

Forsythe had had enough. He was on his feet and heading toward the hall. Over his shoulder he flung back a few words. "I'm *not* in the habit of evaluating my hostess's possessions."

There was no answer and as he threw open the door he noticed that Dowling had picked up the Georgian teapot and was engrossed in its silver luster. Whether he was admiring the reflection of his manly features or assessing its market value, Forsythe neither knew or cared.

CHAPTER FOUR

Forsythe slowly mounted the staircase to the first floor. He felt chilled, his leg was stiff and sore, and his head ached dully. This was shaping up as a trying weekend and, despite the presence of Erika Von Farr, he regretted letting Sandy talk him into it.

On the landing he found Potter, who took him in hand, introduced him to an upstairs maid who was an older edition of the pert little girl Forsythe had glimpsed on his arrival, and finally ushered him into a large comfortable bedroom.

"About dinner," the barrister queried, "I understand dress is informal."

"Extremely, sir. The, ah, gentlemen connected with films generally wear those denim trousers, although the ladies do make some effort. Miss Honoria always dresses, sir. I took the liberty of laying out your dark suit. The bathroom is located at the end of the hall and if you should require anything further, ring for Sarah."

"Are the maids related?"

"Sisters, sir, and newly arrived to help with the guests. Mrs. Potter and I are getting a bit beyond our prime."

A masterful understatement, Forsythe thought, as the butler made his laborious departure. He sought the bath, found the hot water supply as erratic as Dowling had predicted, and, taking Potter's gentle hint, donned the black suit that the officious Mrs. Meeks had slipped into his case.

When he answered the dinner bell he was glad he had dressed. Giles, Borthwick, and Cochrane had merely exchanged sweatshirts for sport shirts but Dowling had changed into designer jeans and a blue silk shirt with a matching scarf at his noble throat. The actor's clothes might have been casual but they were costly. Touches of gold accented his costume, a Patek watch on one wrist, a link bracelet on the other, a glint of gold plating on his belt buckle. To carry out the blue theme, Forsythe was amused to notice deeper blue points peeking from a silk breast pocket. The ladies had made notable efforts. Marcia had discarded her white suit and was wearing a peach dress of similar elegance; Miss Sanderson looked well in crisp green; and Honoria Farquson was resplendent in a vintage and fussy dinner dress that happily echoed the color of her cornflower eyes.

It was Erika who caught and held most of the attention. She was dressed simply in something black and filmy that reminded Forsythe of a modified harem costume. She wore no jewelry and her face was innocent of makeup but she'd loosened her hair and it fell around her face and shoulders as softly and darkly as the chiffon flowed around her body. Candlelight was kind to everyone, but for Erika it was a perfect setting and Forsythe had difficulty tearing his eyes from her. He noted that Giles Eady was having the same difficulty.

Dinner proved to be unexpectedly pleasant. Potter, with the assistance of the shy little maid, wavered about serving course after course of the most delicious food the barrister had ever tasted. He'd expected the strains and bickering of

37

the afternoon to continue but harmony reigned. All the film company, including Marcia, exerted themselves to be pleasant. Dowling, seated on Honoria Farquson's right, turned his considerable charm on that lady.

Forsythe applied himself to lobster bisque and covert scrutiny of Erika. For a time conversation was general but in the lull while the soup plates were removed, Forsythe said, "I had always thought of you as an American, Erika, but I understand your parents were English."

"I suppose I'm a true cosmopolitan, Robert." Erika laughed. "I was conceived in England, born in Italy, raised in California."

"Italy?"

"Santa Vittoria," Dowling told Forsythe. "Picturesque little place but it seemed deadly dull."

"A quiet village," Honoria agreed. "You've been there, Mr. Dowling?"

"Passed through it. Last summer. I did stop to try and pick up a souvenir for Erika but everything was gimcrackery and ridiculously overpriced."

Erika turned toward her aunt. "I know so little about how my mother and father met and married, Aunt Honoria. By the time I was old enough to be curious about the past, mother was . . . well, reticent on the subject."

"My fault." Honoria sighed heavily. "Von—her name was Veronica but she was always called Von—we had a dreadful and foolish quarrel when I learned she intended to put you in that first film. You were so young, only eight, and I'm afraid I said unforgivable things. I wrote and accused Von of fulfilling her own ambitions in your life. I hesitate to say this but Von was never a really good actress, dear."

"She knew that. Mother always said she was barely competent and that her brother Erik had all the acting ability in their family."

38

Soft color glowed becomingly in Honoria's face. "He had. If Erik had lived he would have been a great actor. He had the depth, the passion, the courage . . . it was a great pity he died so young. For years I've bitterly regretted not making up the quarrel with your mother. Von refused to write and I would have liked to have gone to Los Angeles and . . . I'm sure if I had we would have made up. But I couldn't leave the colonel and by the time he'd passed on, Von was dead." She sighed again. "We should really make time for the people we love."

Sam Cochrane's bass chimed in. "We all do it, Honoria. All of us live with guilty memories of not making time when we should have."

His eyes, which had been darting from one object to another, suddenly steadied and focused on Michael Dowling. Those words and Cochrane's gaze had an immediate and rather surprising effect on the actor. The salad fork dropped from his hand and Forsythe could have sworn the younger man shivered.

Erika was speaking to her aunt again. "I'm sure mother loved you and was unhappy about your quarrel too."

"I had no business to interfere, dear, but I was concerned about the effect on a little girl. Child actresses sometimes have difficult lives."

"I can't really picture life as being any different, Aunt Honoria. I was truly a movie brat. From the time I was on pabulum I was on a set. Mother took me with her—"

"But who looked after you?"

"Anyone who was handy. Script girls, wardrobe women, makeup people, anyone who was handy. It was a colorful exciting life for a child and I've never regretted it." Erika looked pleadingly at the older woman. "Do tell me about mother and father and Uncle Erik."

"Later, my dear, perhaps after dinner. I shouldn't want to weary my other guests."

Surprisingly it was Dowling who told her warmly, "We'd be enchanted to hear about them, dear lady."

Honoria glanced doubtfully around the table and the other guests made murmurs of agreement. "Very well, but if I become too wordy do tell me. Where shall I start, Erika?"

"At the beginning, please."

"That's a long time ago but . . . My mother was a great deal younger than the colonel and she died at my birth. If she had lived I've often thought Charles and I might have been different people. I only know mother through other people's memories. Charles was four years older than I and he rememberd a bit about her and, of course, the Potters were devoted to her."

"Did grandfather not tell you about your mother?"

"The colonel never mentioned her. I have often fantasized that he loved her deeply and that's why he was rather unkind to me—"

"Bosh!" Marcia Mather said. "My father was her doctor and he said all the colonel wanted from his wife was an heir and a housekeeper. The colonel was *naturally* unkind."

"*De mortius*," Honoria chided gently. "Regardless of his reasons I'm afraid my childhood was a lonely one. There was my brother and the Potters and after a time Teresa and you, Marcia, but father refused to send me away to school and I took lessons in this house with a governess. I remember weeping when you and Teresa went to school. There were vacation times and those were happy days but then Charles and the other two musketeers would go back to school and I would be alone again. As I grew older it became lonelier. The young people had their own lives and when I was eighteen I found I'd lost them."

"Teresa had married husband number one," Marcia mused. "And I was touring with my first play." Candlelight and memory softened her features and her voice had no

40

touch of its usual acerbity. "Charles . . . he'd had a row with the colonel and left, hadn't he?"

"My brother had always rebelled against the colonel, by fits and starts that is. Charles was as terrified of father as I was but he was a boy and that made a difference. This argument was the worst they'd ever had. The colonel threatened disinheritance and Charles fought back and it ended with my brother flinging out of the house and going to London. To make his fortune, he said."

"Just how did he propose to do that?" Marcia asked. "Charles certainly wasn't outstanding at school and he had no profession, did he?"

"No, Charles wasn't brainy and the quarrel with the colonel was about a profession. The colonel wanted my brother to follow in his own footsteps and take a military career. Charles refused. The colonel had also picked out a wife for my brother, a county girl who was a wonderful horsewoman. Charles insisted she should be as she looked, exactly like one of her mounts. So, they had a tearing row and my brother left."

Miss Sanderson had finished her salad and was regarding her hostess with interest. "Teresa said you spent some time in London, Honoria."

Honoria watched the dish of grilled trout being shakily handed around by the butler and then she confided, "A little over a month. That was Charles's doing. Father wouldn't allow my brother to see me or correspond with me but I arranged a mail drop—"

"Like the secret mail drop we had when we were children?" Marcia's long-lashed eyes looked into the past and a small smile tugged at the corners of her painted lips. "Do you remember, Honoria? We pledged ourselves to secrecy and the Three Musketeers signed a solemn vow in blood. Funny, I never have broken that vow."

"Neither have I, dear. And it wasn't in blood. Teresa

41

wouldn't prick her finger and I believe we ended up signing in tomato paste. Charles arranged a simpler way of corresponding with me. He sent his letters to the Potters. He was fond of me and worried about me alone with the colonel so he'd spoken to our Aunt Maud—"

"I remember her. The colonel's only sister. She looked much like him."

"She did look like the colonel but she wasn't the least like him. Aunt Maud agreed to write her brother asking I be sent to her in London, pleading illness. She sent a lovely letter telling him she needed me, I'd be such a comfort and could read to her and so on. The colonel didn't want to let me go but he had to. And so—" Honoria's eyes shone like blue stars— "I left home and went to London."

"And there you met my mother and uncle," Erika breathed.

"Such an exciting time, dear. Here I was a country mouse and plunged straight into what the colonel would call bohemia. Charles had become enthralled with the stage and through it had met Veronica and Erik Larsen. He was living in their tiny flat and had fallen in love with Von. They made room for me and it was close quarters. Three tiny rooms and only one bedroom. Von and I slept there and Erik and Charles bedded down on a daybed in the sitting room." Honoria's laugh tinkled with remembered mirth. "What a wonderful world. How free! I had visions of becoming an actress and watched all their rehearsals. Both Erik and Von had small parts in a play and Charles was working as a stagehand with it."

"Mother and father were married," Erika said dreamily.

"Von was wild about my brother and although he loved her he was as vacillating as he was with the colonel. One moment Charles was all for marrying, the next he was worrying about being cut off without a penny and how he would make a living. But Von was decisive and she got all the licenses and made the arrangements and one day when we drank a great deal of wine she acted. Charles was tiddly and proposing again and before we knew it Erik and I were witnesses and they were married."

Erika's high brow crinkled in thought. "Do you think father regretted it?"

Her aunt took a sip of wine. "I must speak honestly. Perhaps Charles would have in time but there was no time. For two weeks the four of us were wild with happiness and then . . . then Charles and Erik were both dead. Charles had bought a motorbike and there was an accident. The colonel always insisted the boys had been intoxicated but they weren't. I was there and I know."

"After the accident—what did grandfather do?"

Honoria bent her bright head. "He came to London and brought me home. He refused to attend his son's funeral and he wouldn't even speak to Von. One should not speak ill of the dead but he was a bitter, unforgiving man."

Her niece gave her a searching look. "And you went with him?"

"I had no choice. I'd been raised and conditioned to absolute obedience. I no sooner would've disobeyed him at that point than I'd have disobeyed God. But then he went too far and for the first and last time in my life I rebelled."

"What did he do?"

"Von sent me a letter—again by the Potters—and told me she was pregnant. I took it immediately to the colonel. He was outraged that Charles had married an actress but he had a strong feeling for the family line. He'd thought it had ended when my brother died. Now he had a chance for a grandson. He went to Von, reconciled with her, and brought her back here. I was so happy to see her. I loved . . ." Honoria's voice broke.

Reaching past Borthwick, Erika patted her aunt's hand. "If it's too painful, don't go on."

43

Honoria dabbed at her eyes. "The pain should be past. This was over thirty years ago. No, I'll finish. The colonel started on Von, telling her what she could do, what she couldn't. He made plans for her and for her baby. He was dictatorial. But Von was not a Charles or an Honoria. She was a high-spirited, independent girl. Von fought back and the colonel threatened to disinherit both her and her child." She gave a shaky laugh. "Von made a most improper suggestion as to what the colonel could do with his money and he ordered her out. I went with her."

Erika beamed at the older woman. "You finally did rebel."

"A short rebellion. But, yes, Von and I went to the Continent. She'd had a little insurance from her brother Erik and I borrowed some money from Aunt Maud and we went. We lived cheaply in hostels and took buses and trains. Once in a while fellow travelers would give us rides in their cars. Although both of us mourned our dead we were young and Von's pregnancy didn't bother her. We were in Germany and France and Switzerland and then we went to Rome. It was frightfully expensive there and suffocatingly hot. A nice German couple offered us a ride and we went north with them. By that time Von was close to term and very heavy and uncomfortable. When we reached Santa Vittorio she wasn't feeling at all well and so we stayed there. At that time the only inn was terrible and the local doctor, who spoke fluent English, took pity on us and took us into his own house." Honoria looked fondly at Erika's vivid face. "And that was where you were born."

"And then mother took me to the States and you went back to grandfather. Why on earth did you return?"

"Von begged me to go with her to Los Angeles. She said we could get jobs in films and raise you. I was going to borrow more money from Aunt Maud and go and then a wire arrived about the colonel. He'd had a heart attack and it sounded as though he was at death's door. I *had* to return. It was my duty. When I got home I found he was not ill at all. But that was the end of my freedom."

"Aunt Honoria, grandfather lived for twenty-nine years. Why didn't you break away and come to mother and me?"

"I wanted to. Ever so many times I thought I'll go but then the colonel would become ill or pretend he was and I'd think, I'll go as soon as he's well enough to leave. Time passed and then Von and I had that silly quarrel about you, dear, and it was too late . . ."

Erika was resting her chin on her palm, misty dark hair falling forward across the classic lines of cheekbones. "Did the colonel—grandfather—never want to see me?"

Her aunt hesitated and then said slowly, "I'm afraid not. If you had been a boy the colonel would have struggled to take you away from your mother. But he didn't . . . he had little use for girls. But you were valued, my dear, by your mother, by me. You were most precious to both of us." Honoria glanced up at the butler, who was hovering over her chair. "Oh, Potter. Is it that time already? Yes, do have coffee served in the drawing room." She gave a little laugh. "I'm afraid people who are much alone tend to be garrulous when they have a chance to talk. You must forgive me. I've monopolized you."

Dowling sprang to help her up. "Dear lady, you've been absolutely enthralling." He offered an arm to Honoria, the other to her niece, and led the way to the drawing room. Forsythe and Miss Sanderson were the last to leave. In a low voice Miss Sanderson asked her employer, "What do you think of our hostess?"

"Reading between the lines of life with father I'd say she should receive a nomination for sainthood."

Coffee and brandy were being served but Dowling waved them away, took Honoria's arm and said jovially, "I was wondering, auntie—"

She pulled away and said sharply, "Don't call me that, Mr. Dowling."

"What *am* I to call you? Miss Farquson seems unsuitable." He flashed perfect teeth. "Let's take a turn in the garden and discuss it."

"If you wish." She paused to scoop up a cardigan, draped it around her shoulders, and beamed at her guests. "I know this is a working weekend for you but I do feel you should have a little relaxation. If the weather is fine tomorrow I've planned a treat. A picnic on the river. I can borrow a boat and—"

"I must decline," Giles said hastily. "I'll be working all day."

"Nonsense. All work and no play, Mr. Eady. We'll discuss it later."

The writer wandered to the window and looked up at the sky. "Seems to be clouding over. Maybe we'll get lucky and have a downpour. I'll offer up a small prayer."

"You don't care for picnics?" Miss Sanderson asked.

"Loathe them. Never could see why anyone would want to sit on the ground and share their food with insects." He took another glance out into the darkened garden. "Can't figure why Mickey Darling is showering our hostess with attention. Yesterday he hardly knew she was around."

Forsythe could have hazarded a guess but it was Marcia Mather who snapped, "Our boy doesn't do anything without a good reason."

The other actress had picked up a magazine and was leafing through it. She flung it down and whirled to face the older woman. "Must you always be suspicious? Mickey is simply being kind to my aunt."

"He'd have to look up the word 'kind' in the dictionary."

Hastily Borthwick asked the writer, "How did you get along with the rewrite, Giles?"

"Only had enough time to look it over. What you need is

46

a magician, not a writer. Can you imagine Heathcliff raving on about his identity, his inner being? The audience is going to be rolling in the aisles." Giles slouched over and lowered his lanky body in a chair near Erika. "I think you'd better consider this carefully, love. If this film goes ahead on schedule you're in a fair way of having your career ruined. Your fans may have stood still for that first film with Mickey but with this one they'll be running for the exits. Even the devoted ones like Robert here will be—"

"I don't want to hear any more!" She presented her back squarely to him.

"I think you'd better listen," Cochrane's deep voice turned all eyes to the shadowed corner where he sat in a wing chair. "Keep in mind the only reason Mel and Giles and I are working on this film is because of you. Mel and I worked with you from the time you were a child. Giles . . . well he wrote his first script for you when you were eighteen or nineteen. Not only are we all fond of you but we respect your talent."

"Mickey and I are going to be married. You can't stop that, Sam."

"We're not trying to. Marry the boy, live with him, do anything you want, but for God's sake don't work with him. Keep your careers separate. You've been in this business for over twenty years. You know what the score is, how fickle the public can be. Now you're a big name but—"

"For God's sake knock off the father act!" Erika flung her head back, long hair swirling around her shoulders. "You haven't the track record for it. After what happened to Jenny—"

Erika stopped abruptly, the angry color draining from her features, leaving them pallid and stricken. Forsythe glanced around. All of the other people, including Miss Sanderson, looked appalled. He couldn't discern Cochrane's expression but lamplight fell across the huge hands. They were bunched into fists.

"Sam." The girl went to the cameraman's side and stood, every fluid line of her body whispering contriteness, the outstretched hand mutely imploring forgiveness. "Sam, I'm so ashamed . . . I didn't mean . . . Sam . . ."

For a moment the big man was immobile and then the fist relaxed and he reached out to pat the girl's hip. "You're right, little girl, I don't qualify as a father or even as an advisor. Do what you want. It's your life."

For moments no one moved or spoke. Marcia raised her handkerchief and it looked as if she were wiping her eyes. Then Mickey came bolting in through the window and Forsythe, this time, was glad to see him. The actor stood in a dramatic pose, pointing at the window, and when Honoria stepped into the room he scooped her up and hugged her to his side. "Pay attention, people; I have an announcement. Come here, Erika." Reaching out a long arm he pulled her against his other side. "This is the happiest moment of my life—"

"God," Marcia groaned, "he's going to make another speech."

"Not even you can rile me right now, Marcia. So shut up, you're wasting your time. On Monday when we get back to London Erika and I are going to be married. Aunt Honoria—" White teeth flashed down at Honoria and she smiled back— "has given her blessing. It will be a small wedding. No time to fuss and those big affairs are a waste of money but there'll be a reception and you're all invited. Even you, Marcia—"

"Thanks but no thanks."

The white smile faltered and then reappeared. "Suit yourself. There's more news. Not only has Aunt Honoria consented but she's giving us an unbelievable wedding present. Erika, this house and estate is to be ours!"

"No," Erika tore herself loose from his arm and went to her aunt. "We can't accept that. This is your home."

"Don't be a little ninny," her lover told her. "This is what your aunt wants."

Gently Honoria detached herself from Dowling's grasp and embraced her niece. "It's my wish, dear. I can't possibly keep this place on. I simply haven't the funds and the Potters are beyond heavy work. We'll be cozy in a little cottage. Besides, this was your father's home, and his father's and . . . way back to your ancestors. You will want to keep it on, Erika, and raise your children here?"

"Oh, yes," Erika breathed.

Perhaps she means it, Forsythe brooded, but as soon as Dowling has his hands on it the old family home will blossom into a housing estate. You *damn* fool, he berated himself, you're responsible for this. Your big heedless mouth!

"I'm so happy!" Erika cried and burst into tears.

"Women," Dowling said indulgently.

The girl put out her hand blindly. "Hankie, darling."

He fumbled through his pockets. "Sorry. Aunt Honoria, do you have one?"

She was searching through the pockets of her cardigan. Paper crinkled and she laughed. "Only a shopping list. Marcia?"

Marcia was blowing her nose. "She wouldn't want mine."

Uncoiling himself from his chair, Giles produced a crisp white square and stepped to the girl's side. He tilted her chin up and tenderly blotted tears from her cheeks. Still holding her face up, he murmured, "I'm going to be the first one to kiss the bride." He bent and pressed his lips to hers. It wasn't a fleeting kiss, it was prolonged. There was passion in that kiss and Erika was wriggling to free herself but Giles held her firmly.

Forsythe's attention snapped to Dowling. An unbecoming color mottled the bronzed features and his hands knotted into fists. He raised an arm and Forsythe thought, now we're going to have fisticuffs. Borthwick hastened to intervene. Tapping Giles's shoulder, he said lightly, "My turn," as though asking for a dance. The young man's hands dropped away and Borthwick lightly kissed Erika.

The girl whirled toward Cochrane. "Are you going to wish us well, Sam?"

Picking her up like a doll, the big man brushed his lips across her brow. "I wish you well, little girl; I wish you the best. You deserve it."

He didn't mention what Dowling deserved and none of the other men were offering to shake hands with the prospective groom. Ignoring the actor, Miss Sanderson hugged Erika and then Honoria. Marcia Mather hadn't moved and was staring steadily at the wall. To Forsythe's surprise, Erika ran over to him and brushed her lips over his cheek. It felt like being kissed by a flower, he thought, and that was what the girl smelled like. Fresh and innocent and fragrant. For moments after that kiss he noticed nothing and then he snapped back and heard Dowling demanding champagne.

"I'm afraid we don't have any, Mickey," Honoria told him. Mickey Darling's mouth was arranging itself into a pout. She hastened to add, "First thing tomorrow I'll send to the village for several bottles. For now, we'll have wine. Potter, will you get a bottle, please? The colonel kept a good cellar and we still have some excellent vintages."

Miss Sanderson said, "None for me. I'm afraid I had a bit much with dinner. I'm going to stretch my legs before bed. Robby?"

"I'll join you."

They stepped into the garden and a fresh, cool breeze greeted them. A full moon threw silvery light and grotesque shadows and there was a scattering of stars but Giles had been right. Clouds were piling up ominously in the west. For moments they walked silently and then Forsythe said, "Better get it off your chest."

"Is she out of her mind?" Miss Sanderson exploded.

"By she I suppose you mean the estimable Miss Farquson."

"All she has is this estate and she's going to hand it over to that . . . that colossal ass."

"I take it you're not one of the multitude of Mickey Darling fans."

"I detest him. He's like something that crawls out from under a stone. A cockroach!"

Forsythe grinned down at her. "I doubt whether cockroaches live under stones. Perhaps you're thinking of a beetle."

"How can you take it so lightly? Oh, I know you don't know any of them but you seem to like Honoria."

"I do and I'm not taking it lightly. Your bigmouthed employer is the one who put Mickey on the trail. Explained to him this afternoon that this would be a dandy place for a housing estate."

"Don't feel badly, Robby. In time he'd have figured that out himself. Funny, I got here when the film group was arriving—Marcia was the only one who came early—and I'd have sworn Honoria had the same reaction to Dowling that I did. Then she makes a complete swingaround and gives him everything she has."

It was Forsythe's turn to console. "Don't blame her. He was doing a job on her tonight that few women could have resisted and as he says himself, he has a way with the fair sex." He touched her elbow. "Over here. Let's sit and let the beauty of the night soothe our savage breasts."

She sank down on the stone bench and appeared to be studying the distorted shadow thrown by a hawthorn.

51

"Dowling was telling you about his women? Did he mention Marcia Mather?"

"Chapter and verse."

"Any other?"

"A teacher he conned into funding his trip to Hollywood and a woman agent he used to get his start in films. A sordid tale but one he viewed with pride to say nothing of satisfaction."

"Completely immoral. I've heard people described that way but he's the first one I've ever met. All he cares about is his slimy skin. And money, of course. He likes expensive trinkets but he's unbelievably cheap."

"You sound as though you're an authority on Michael Dowling."

"I am. Marcia has told me all. Of course I suppose one should be cautious. She practically bubbles over with venom."

"Care to share the details?"

"No!" She softened her refusal. "Robby, some things are best left alone."

"As you wish." Knowing the best way to elicit information from his secretary, Forsythe took out his pipe and proceeded to fill it.

As usual, an appearance of disinterest worked. Miss Sanderson gave him a sidelong look, studied the long fingers deftly packing tobacco into the carved bowl of the pipe, and then asked, "Did you notice Dowling's reaction to Sam Cochrane?"

"Only one incident." He shielded a match and drew lustily on the pipe.

"Which was?" she prompted.

"At dinner. Cochrane made some platitude about people never taking time for the ones they love and looked at Dowling. Mickey had an odd reaction."

"Well, he should. Marcia told me—and bear in mind she

hates him—that there's a possibility that Dowling was implicated in Sam's daughter's death. Her name was Jenny—"

"Ah, the name Erika blurted out and then wished she hadn't."

"She was sixteen, hooked on heroin, and pregnant. Marcia didn't seem eager to give details. For a woman of her type she seemed rather emotional about it. But she did say many people thought Dowling was responsible for the child's corruption."

Forsythe shook his head. "That I can't believe. I don't mean the child's death. That kind of tragedy is far from rare. But I can't picture Cochrane working with his daughter's corruptor."

"Neither can I. But Marcia said it's all rumor, no proof. Then there was Beth Borthwick—"

"The director's daughter?"

"His wife. And this isn't rumor, it's fact. Seems Mel was devoted to his wife, why Marcia couldn't see. Mel is surrounded by pretty actresses and it seems Beth was far from pretty. Marcia said she was a dumpy little woman, looked like a brown mouse."

"Doesn't sound like Mickey's type."

"She wasn't and apparently he didn't seem to know she was alive until she came into an inheritance from a grandmother. Then he noticed her and swept her off her feet. Marcia tells me Dowling has a weird effect on even sensible women. Almost hypnotizes them. Little mouse Beth didn't have a chance."

"Was Borthwick aware of the affair?"

"Very much but he was tolerant about it. Theatrical people appear to take that sort of thing rather philosophically. Marcia said Mel thought it would wear off but then Dowling had to go to France on location for one of his films and Beth followed him without even leaving a note for her husband. A couple of months later Mel heard that Dowling had walked out on Beth, leaving her stranded in a hotel in Cannes. Mel went hotfooting over to retrieve his wife—" Miss Sanderson broke off and twisted a handkerchief in her hands. "When Mel got there he found Beth had chucked herself off her hotel balcony. This time she did leave a note. Told Mel how Mickey had treated her, draining her inheritance, and then walking out. She said she was so humiliated she no longer wanted to live."

Forsythe's pipe had gone out but he made no move to relight it. He stared at his secretary. "And Borthwick is working with Dowling, placating him . . . What kind of man *is* he?"

"Hotheaded, according to Marcia Mather. She said at that moment Mel would have killed Dowling if he could have gotten his hands on him. But that was four years ago. As for Borthwick working with Dowling—he's doing it for the same reason Sam and Giles are. They all have an emotional involvement with Erika Von Farr and Marcia said they're trying to get her to see reason and drop Dowling. Marcia says Giles is deeply in love with the girl and has been for years."

Forsythe remembered the agonized emotion on the writer's freckled face when the young actress had touched his arm. "I fear I'll never understand show business, Sandy. Here we have three people, four counting Marcia, who all have good reason to twist Dowling's neck and they're not only working closely with him but letting him call the shots. I really can't see Sam Cochrane doing this. He strikes me as a man who could be dangerous. How long ago did his daughter Jenny die?"

"Marcia didn't say. The way she spoke, it was only a few months ago."

"Curiouser and curiouser. Does Honoria Farquson know about Dowling's past?"

"Marcia said when she met Honoria in London she told all."

"And what was her reaction?"

"Honoria put it down to gossip and jealousy. And she might be right. As I said Marcia is so full of venom she could be exaggerating." Miss Sanderson shivered and tugged her sweater closer.

"Chilly, Sandy?"

"Uneasy and I've been that way since I arrived." She turned and impulsively squeezed his arm. "I'll admit I was glad to see you, Robby."

He sighed. "Going fey again?"

"You don't *go* fey. I simply get feelings. Remember the one I had in Calvert's studio."

"Vividly."

"And I was right that time." Her pale eyes sought the equally pale moon. "There are undercurrents here, Robby—"

"I'm not surprised. Considering the tangled relationships among this group it would be strange if there weren't."

"It's not just that. It's—" She broke off and got up abruptly. "What's the use? I am cold and I'm going in."

Forsythe grinned up at her. "Allow me to put your feelings into words. 'I could a tale unfold whose lightest word, Would harrow thy soul, freeze thy young blood—'"

"My blood isn't young," she snapped. "You and your quotations. Honestly, Robby, you'd think you had sole rights to Hamlet. Try this one and it isn't Shakespeare, so you'll never pin it.

> Her lips were red, her looks were free
> Her locks were yellow as gold:
> Her skin was white as leprosy,
> The Night-mare Life-in-Death was she,
> Who thicks a man's blood with cold.

"What is that supposed to signify?"

She threw him an icy look. "You figure it out, detective."

"Let's see . . . who do I know with locks of yellow gold?"

"Don't be so damned literal." Turning on her heels, she strode toward the house.

The barrister called after her, "Got it, Sandy! Coleridge and the Ancient Mariner."

She muttered something that sounded suspiciously like "Get stuffed" and stepped over the threshold of the long window.

CHAPTER FIVE

LONG AFTER MISS SANDERSON HAD LEFT, THE BARRISTER remained in the garden, staring unseeingly at the play of shadows, his pipe clutched in his hand. Then he realized he was chilled and glanced up at the moon. It was almost veiled by a bank of clouds. He got to his feet and lurched, grasping at the back of the bench for support. That ruddy leg again, but it was his fault. The cement seat was too cold to have sat on for so long. Rubbing his thigh, he limped into the house. Only one lamp was lit, shedding barely enough light for him to circle around the furniture. When he opened the door to the hall he found stronger light, and his hostess, who was rounding a corner that he presumed led to the kitchen. She was carrying a loaded tray.

"Allow me," he said and took it from her.

"So kind of you. Did you enjoy your walk, Mr. Forsythe? I notice you're limping."

"An old injury and I managed to get chilled."

"I have a heating pad in my room if you'd care for it."

"No, by morning I'll be fine."

They'd reached the landing and Honoria led the way

down the hall. The lighting was subdued here also and caught her hair with a nimbus. Idly Forsythe wondered if this could be the deadly lady from Coleridge's poem. No, Honoria's hair was more silver than gold. She paused at a door opposite his own and he noticed the door was ajar. She switched on lights. "Please put the tray over there. Yes, on the desk will be fine."

He set the tray down carefully and stood back to admire the desk. "Sheraton?"

"My great-grandmother's and a piece I'm fond of. I must make room for it in my cottage. I can't bear to leave it." She looked at the towering four-poster and sighed. "So few things will be able to go with us."

"Will you regret leaving here?"

"Yes and no. I can't say I've had a happy life in this house but it's all I know. I see you've discovered my table of memorabilia, Mr. Forsythe."

"I didn't mean to pry."

"You're certainly not. I'm proud of my souvenirs and I know you admire my niece. As you see I have eight portraits of Erika as a little girl. Von was very good about it." Tenderly the woman touched a small object. "These were Erika's first shoes. Her mother had them bronzed and sent them to me. On every birthday Von sent me a portrait of Erika and when the child was old enough she always encouraged Erika to send a small gift. I've always loved dogs and Erika selected these little china replicas all by herself. And speaking of dogs, here's my Ciara." A shaggy little animal had crawled out of a wicker basket and was rubbing against Honoria's ankles. She scooped the Cairn terrier up and hugged it.

Forsythe patted Ciara's head and the lips promptly pulled back from tiny sharp teeth. "Neither Heathcliff nor Ciara are friendly."

Honoria laughed. "When you get to know Heathcliff he's

a powder puff. Ciara is quite old and inclined to be grounchy. I must admit she never has been found of anyone but Potty—I call Mrs. Potter that—and me. She doesn't even like Potter and he's most kind to her." Honoria looked affectionately down at the dog and added, "In some ways Potty and Ciara are much alike. Both old and rather irritable but protective and devoted to me. Take that tray for instance. Ever since I can remember Potty's made up a tray for me each night. She seems to feel I don't get enough nourishment. However, it is nice to be fussed over even if one does feel like a child at times. I see you're looking at my favorite picture of Erika, Mr. Forsythe."

The barrister had drifted back to the table and was regarding an early picture of Erika. She had been an enchanting child. Dimpled hands clutched a large teddy bear and elf locks fell over huge solemn eyes. He spoke his thoughts aloud, "A lovely child."

"She was four in that portrait. I did so love the child. When we met again recently I was surprised at the initial lack of warmth I felt for her. Still, when one considers that Erika is now a woman and I know little about her I suppose it is understandable."

Honoria was looking distressed and Forsythe hastened to comfort her. "She must have seemed a stranger. In time affection will come."

"Yes, I believe it will. These last few days . . . I already feel much different. Ah, I see you've spotted my brother's wedding picture." One hand detached itself from the dog and she picked up a faded picture in a silver frame. "We couldn't afford a good photographer and this isn't too clear but here is my brother Charles."

Forsythe looked down at the young man with his arm around a slender dark girl. There was a strong resemblance to his sister but his chin and mouth were weaker. The young

59

Honoria had been incredibly lovely, with a quality of dewy innocence. "Your brother looked so much like you."

"We both took after our mother. She was Danish, an au pair girl when the colonel met her. Charles and I inherited our coloring from her." Honoria smiled. "Charles hated his hair. At school boys called him Whitey. Erika looks much like her mother, doesn't she?"

"And her uncle. This man is Erik Larsen, isn't he?"

"Yes, that's Erik. Sad he died so young. A splendid young man and what an actor he would have made." Replacing the silver-framed picture, Honoria lifted the one of Erika at four. "The child so resembles her father." She added, "Not in looks, in nature. Now, Mr. Forsythe, are you certain I can't lend you a heating pad for your leg?"

"I don't need it, Miss Farquson, but if you have any books I would like to borrow one. I have a case of books in the car but I don't really want to go out again. Anything would do. I read myself to sleep."

She was stooping to tuck the old dog back in its basket. "I'm sorry, I have no books here. I usually do my reading in the colonel's library. He was a great reader, mainly of military history, but there is a selection of classics and I've added some modern novels. Do help yourself." She straightened. "Please leave the door ajar. Ciara is so funny now, she hates the door closed. Becomes quite restless and nervous. And, Mr. Forsythe, I'd like to say how happy I am that you are able to be with us this weekend."

"And I," the barrister lied gallantly, "am delighted to be here."

As he made his way along the hall and down the stairs he told himself that wasn't wholly a lie. As far as his hostess and her fascinating niece was concerned he *was* delighted. As for the rest of the guests, particularly Michael Dowling, well, that was another matter.

The library was directly across from the dining room and

when Forsythe opened the door he found Giles Eady behind the desk, pounding the keys of a portable. In the powerful light from the desk lamp his freckled face was drawn and weary.

"Sorry," Forsythe said. "Didn't realize you were still working."

"Time I knocked off." Giles pulled a sheet from the typewriter and put it on top of a pile of yellow sheets. "Beastly job. Hey, Robert, how do you like this bit of Dowling-inspired dialogue? 'I am a complex man and my love is twisted and devious. Catherine, you will find Heathcliff's love a curse.' I've a feeling Brontë is going to be spinning in her grave." He pulled his lanky frame up and stretched. "What do you think of the colonel's sanctum sanctorum?"

Forsythe had been looking around the square room. It was full of dark leather, heavy furniture, and dark velvet hangings. "I don't fancy it."

"Must have suited the master, though. There he is, over the mantel, still brooding over his domain."

Colonel Farquson had been painted in uniform and Sandy's memory of him had been accurate. He was handsome in a cold way. The small dark eyes were like chips of ice and there was a touch of cruelty around his lips. Giles wandered over and stood, his hands clasped behind him, gazing up at the painting. "Genus Heathcliff," he mused. "The colonel would have been a natural for that part."

"I think not. Brontë's Heathcliff called for passion, dark and distorted granted, but definitely passion. There's not a trace of passion in that face."

"You're right. Odd I didn't spot that. You're a quick study on faces, Robert." Giles swung around to face the older man. "Is that the barrister or the detective speaking?"

"Neither. Simple observation."

"Let me put you to the test. You met our little group only today." Giles drummed his knuckles on the desk. "I won't give you the easy ones. Anyone could spot Marcia as shallow and vain and spiteful. I'll give you a tough one. Sam Cochrane."

Forsythe humored the writer. "When I first met Cochrane I compared him with Heathcliff, the four-legged one. But on closer study I'd say the man is more like a rhino, huge and slow, but if he ever charged I'd hate to be in the path."

"Excellent. Now, the golden boy, Mickey Darling."

Forsythe's recent conversation with Miss Sanderson compelled him to say, "Either he's incredibly brave or unbelievably stupid."

"You batted out. The lad is neither brave nor stupid. Dowling's shrewd, or at least, he has a type of low cunning. Try Mel Borthwick."

"The opposite of Cochrane. Quick thinking, quick moving. Probably competent."

"Good. The magical Miss Farr."

Forsythe tired of the game. "She's too complex for me."

A wide grin lighted Giles's tired face. "You batted out again. Erika's the simplest of the lot." He watched the barrister as he moved along the ranks of books. "Unless you like Napoleonic history you're wasting your time in that section. The Crimean War is right below it and the Second World War to the right. Over there are a bunch of light romances, our hostess's contribution I would imagine, and at the end are a scattering of classics. There're two copies of *Wuthering Heights* if you're in the mood."

"Not tonight. I want to rest and I'm afraid I might have nightmares of motorbikes and jeans to say nothing of helmets against a background of moors." Running a finger over the line of classics, Forsythe asked idly, "How do you read Miss Farquson's face?"

"She certainly is nothing like her father."

"Her mother was Danish."

"Ah, that's where the Nordic coloring comes from. A descendant of the Vikings." Again the attractive grin flashed. "Let me put it this way. If I'd been around thirty years ago and the right age I'd have snapped that lady up. I don't believe in fairy tales but I've a hunch she would have given a man the happy ever after. Too bad she never married."

"See any trace of her in her niece?"

"Nary a one. Maybe Erika's the one who takes after grandfather. Ah, I see you've picked a book. What is it? *L'Assommoir*? Isn't Zola a bit horrific and oppressive for bedtime reading?"

"The horror and oppression was long ago. The only horror that concerns me is today's and tomorrow's."

"How true." Giles thumped the pile of yellow sheets. "Now here's complete horror. Care for a nightcap? All I have is brandy. If you hunger for whiskey you'll have to appeal to Mickey."

"From the little I've seen of him it would be a waste of time. Does he ever share?"

"Only with Erika and that's simply an investment. Goodnight, Robert, sleep tight."

Forsythe headed for bed, a brief session with Zola, and then a deep and dreamless sleep.

CHAPTER SIX

I~N THE MORNING FORSYTHE FOUND GILES EADY'S PRAYER~ had been answered and rain was pelting against the house. When he reached the morning room he found the household breakfasting and the writer, wearing a complacent smile, eating a huge breakfast. Their hostess stood with her back to the room, regarding the rain-drenched garden. Winking at Forsythe, Giles told her, "A shame the rain's spoiling your picnic, Miss Farquson."

"Don't be hypocritical, Mr. Eady. I know you're delighted. As a matter of fact I have an alternative plan. The weather can be uncertain in May, you know. Bright and warm one day and nasty the next."

Giles's smile faded. "Does this plan involve the river and a boat?"

"Of course not." She turned and beamed at them. "You all will enjoy this outing. Our old gardener's grandson has started a business on the family farm. Leslie was a brilliant boy, took all sorts of scholarships, and now has a commercial flower business going. He supplies a number of florist shops in London and—"

"I am not," Giles interrupted, "going to tramp around muddy daffodil fields in the rain."

"Me neither," Marcia said. Her voice was hoarse and the tip of her nose was red and raw. Her makeup was not as perfect as it had been the previous day and she wore a thick tweed skirt and a heavy sweater. "I had a simply dreadful night, feverish, and I could hardly breathe." She'd taken a chair close to the roaring fire and she pointed to the hearth. "Honoria, I'm going to stay right here and keep warm."

"Don't be silly, dear. You can bundle up and you'll be warm where we're going. Mr. Eady, you will not be required to be outdoors at all. As for the daffodils, it's well past their season."

"I think it's a great idea," Dowling said warmly. He was at the sideboard heaping his plate from an assortment of silver-covered dishes on a hotplate.

Honoria said firmly, "I've already rung up Leslie Koster and he's delighted to show us through his greenhouse. The boy is tremendously excited, as Erika is his favorite film star."

"Really?" Dowling didn't sound as warm.

"And his wife Ann worships you, Mickey."

"In that case we can't disappoint the lady. I vote we all go."

Marcia sneezed. "Not me."

At that moment a short woman with the build and bearing of Queen Victoria swept into the room. She swept by Forsythe in a rustle of long black skirts and told her mistress imperiously, "You haven't had a bite of breakfast and you were out walking in that downpour before the day was even started. Sit dowm immediately, Miss Honoria." Honoria meekly obeyed and the cook selected a boiled egg, two rashers of bacon, a slice of toast, and plumped them down before her. "Now eat every scrap." Mrs. Potter calmly accepted compliments on her cooking, raves about the grilled kidney from Dowling, more subdued gratification from Cochrane and Borthwick, and then, with a last admonishment to Honoria, made her regal departure.

Honoria sighed and sliced the top from the egg. "Potty makes me feel about six but she means well."

"She's a marvelous cook," Miss Sanderson said.

"Potty was the only person who seemed to have no fear of the colonel. Remember that summer, Marcia, when we were nine or was it ten and the Three Musketeers had got up to some mischief and—"

"Ten, and the colonel decided Teresa and I were a bad influence on you. He wouldn't let you leave the grounds and we weren't supposed to step onto them. Teresa and I did our best to keep in touch. We sneaked notes to our mail drop telling you about parties and picnics and so on."

"And succeeded in making me feel even worse. I moped around and went off my food and Potty went to the colonel. She told him if I wasn't allowed a normal life and playtime with my friends, Potter and she were handing in their notice. The colonel wasn't worried about Potter but he was terrified of losing a good cook like Potty. He set great store by a good table, you know. So, he had to retract and the musketeers had a wonderful summer."

Erika smiled at her aunt. "Were you really walking in the rain this morning?"

"Before any of you were up. I love walking and rain doesn't bother me at all, in fact, I like it. Now, are we all agreed on our little outing?"

Everyone but Marcia Mather nodded. She stubbornly shook her dark head. Honoria said coaxingly, "I think you will want to come, dear. Leslie does raise flowers commercially but his hobby is experimentation. Would you believe he successfully grafted six different types of roses on one bush? Think of it, *six*."

"I've never cared for roses, Honoria."

"What about orchids?"

Marcia murmured, "Orchids," and looked interested.

She was, Forsythe thought, the perfect type to dote on that fleshy odorless flower.

"Orchids," Honoria repeated. "An entire room devoted to rare species."

"I suppose if I bundled up it would do me no harm. When will we be going?"

"Directly after luncheon," Honoria promised.

That afternoon three cars rolled down the winding driveway and left the Farquson estate. The lead vehicle was a vintage Bentley driven by Honoria with Marcia, muffled to her ears, at her side. In the rear seat were Borthwick and Cochrane. Dowling's sleek Ferrari was next in line and Erika Von Farr, wearing a red anorak that matched the car's color, was his passenger. Forsythe brought up the rear with Miss Sanderson at his side and Giles Eady lounging in the rear seat. Honoria Farquson set a slow pace through Bury-Sutton, where, despite the weather, a number of villagers were moving about. All of them respectfully saluted the Bentley and Honoria, and stared with open curiosity at the Ferrari and the two actors.

Giles chuckled. "Must have set the locals on their ears having two screen idols in their midst. Mickey has been down here soaking in the adulation and possibly charging for autographs. Hauled Erika, much against her will, along with him."

"You're disgustingly cynical," Miss Sanderson chided.

"An occupational hazard."

It was raining even harder. The windshield wipers could hardly keep up with the deluge of water. They passed one of the housing estates, dismal and looking rather squalid, and turned onto a road that, like the one that led to the Farquson house, followed the meandering path of the River Carey. Eventually it ended in a farmyard walled with gray rock, with an ancient stone cottage squarely facing a modern structure built mainly of glass.

"From the looks of this layout I'd say our host is doing pretty well," Giles observed. "Talk about study in contrasts. The past and the present. I rather like the past. That must be Leslie now. Looks more like a doctor than a gardener."

The plump man greeting Honoria was wearing a spotless, high-necked white coat. He had receding hair and huge glasses the thickness of bottle glass. Through these lenses myopic eyes were peering ecstatically at Erika Von Farr. I wonder, Forsythe thought, whether I wore that expression of absolute idiocy when I met her. He decided he probably had. Leslie Koster hurried them into the modern structure and an entrance room provided with clothes hooks along one wall.

"You had better let me take your coats," he told them. "You'll find this building warm, and in the tropical areas uncomfortably so."

They divested themselves of anoraks, topcoats, and raincoats while he beamed at them. Forsythe could see the man was fairly quivering with excitement. "Ordinarily visitors aren't allowed on these premises but because of Miss Farquson and all . . . Anyway, the best way to handle your tour is for me to show you around and then you can wander about by yourselves. If you have any questions I would be delighted to answer them. This way, ladies and gentlemen. As you can see this is actually a complex of rooms. We'll start at this end. There is the rose room, the next is devoted to carnations, and here we have begonias and . . ."

Leslie set a rapid pace and they trailed along behind him through a dazzling display of colors and textures and odors. It was hot enough that Forsythe was tempted to remove his suit coat and he envied Dowling and Erika in jeans and sleeveless tops. Their host had his hand on Erika's arm and appeared to be addressing his remarks solely to her. A scowling Marcia tugged at the white jacket. "Honoria tells me you have orchids."

Without removing his eyes from the other actress's profile, he said, "They're at the far end. Now this area is—"

"What's that?" Borthwick asked. "Some sort of laboratory?"

They clustered around the director. The room he was pointing at was a small but well-fitted laboratory. There was much stainless steel and porcelain and it was spotless. Over a counter was a long shelf bearing bottles with black printing on labels that were large enough to be easily read from the doorway. Glancing at the weak eyes behind the huge lenses, Forsythe decided the huge printing was perhaps necessary. "Looks like the lair of an alchemist," Cochrane said in his deep voice.

"Hardly." Leslie laughed. "I make up my own fertilizers and sprays. With some of the delicate plants it's necessary and it's also cheaper than buying them ready-made."

Marcia moved impatiently. "The orchids."

Their host took a few steps and opened a door. "Right in here, Miss Mather. What do you think of that? It's a particularly fine specimen of Phalaenopsis. Observe the color. This is a Vanya. Over here we have Miltonias and Lycastes."

Leslie continued proudly naming the blooms and Marcia was flitting from one plant to another ahhing and oohing. The blast of air from the room was stifling and Forsythe, who cared little for orchids, backed away. He noticed some of the others were retracing their steps. Pausing, he admired a magnificent hibiscus and noticed with some amusement that their host was in hot pursuit of Erika, who was just disappearing into the rose room. Forsythe lost all track of time in those rooms filled with the glory and perfume of blooms. Vaguely he was aware of other people. Cochrane seemed engrossed in variegated daisies, Miss Sanderson was hovering over enormous shaggy carnations, Dowling was in animated conversation with Leslie Koster, whose spectacles turned steadily toward Erika. Dowling seemed to be pumping their host, not about plants, but about the housing estate they'd recently viewed. "I have no interest in such things," Leslie was saying. "I did receive an offer for this property but turned it down."

Dowling cocked his head. "Seems to me there should be more money in selling than in holding on. After all, you could set up elsewhere."

"Kosters," Leslie snapped, "have farmed this land for generations."

Forsythe didn't wait to hear the argument, sentiment versus business, that ensued. He wandered on, glimpsing Honoria examining hanging fuchsias, and paused by Erika's side. She was touching the petals of a pink rose. He looked, not at the rose, but at her. As bad as Leslie Koster, he thought, but what a magical creature the girl is. Every movement she makes is touched with grace. Poetry, he thought dreamily, a poem in human form. Eyes like limpid pools in which a man could lose his soul. He longed to touch her, to feel poetry beneath his hand. She turned her head, misty hair swirling about her shoulders, and she smiled at him. Her words were prosaic. "You like roses too, Robert?"

"Very much," he told her and forced himself away, down another aisle, into another section.

Cochrane loomed up beside him. "I'm glad we came," he told the barrister and added simply, "This is . . . soothing," and drifted away.

Later, and Forsythe had no idea how much later, he heard Leslie calling their names. He found their host in the doorway of the entrance room. Erika and Honoria were with him and the others were approaching. "Have you seen your fill?" Leslie asked.

"I could never get my fill of orchids," Marcia told him dreamily.

"My wife has prepared tea. She's been excited ever since Miss Farquson rang up. Now, please don't say no. Ann's a fan of yours, Mr. Dowling." Weak eyes examined the actor wonderingly as though looking in vain for the reason for his wife's devotion.

"I never," Dowling told him gallantly, "disappoint a lady."

Coats and jackets were donned and they dashed through pelting rain across the cobbled yard to the cottage. There in a paneled, beamed lounge filled with chintz and copper and, incongruously, Swedish Modern, an elaborate tea was waiting. Waiting also, and completely unnerved by the proximity of her idol, was Ann Koster. She was a round bouncy woman with straight-cut bangs. While they feasted on scones, three different preserves, clotted cream, bread and butter slices, a plate of sausage and ham, and so many small cakes they couldn't be counted, Leslie and Ann produced publicity shots of Erika and Dowling. Marcia Mather ate little and watched morosely as the glossy pictures were autographed. Then Ann, blushing furiously, brought out two movie magazines and showed Dowling articles and pictures across which he indulgently scrawled signatures.

Finally a move was made by Honoria and all of them rose. Their host had disappeared and when they returned to the cars they found what his errand had been. He was carrying a wicker basket and was heedless of the rain flattening thinning hair to his head, drenching his white coat. "Lovely flowers for lovely ladies," he breathed and drank in his lovely lady—Erika.

For Honoria there was an enormous bouquet of long-stemmed roses. She accepted them graciously and as graciously thanked Koster for his time and trouble. Gratefully, Miss Sanderson took a bunch of pink and white carnations. Leslie extended to Marcia a cluster of moist violets in a bed of moss. She looked from her gift to the sheaf of orchids Leslie, with a courtly bow, was presenting to Erika, snorted, and without a word climbed into the Bentley, slamming the door behind her.

The cars rolled out of the yard in reverse order to that in which they'd arrived. The red Ferrari vanished with a cloud of mud and water spurting up from its tires; Forsythe's Rover followed more slowly; and finally, the Bentley, like an aged dowager, made a slow and dignified exit. Miss Sanderson had her long nose buried in the spicy petals of the carnations and Giles no longer lounged in the rear seat but sat bolt upright. "There's going to be hell to pay," he said glumly.

Miss Sanderson removed her nose from the flowers and glanced over her shoulder. "What about?"

"Orchids. Marcia's ready to bite."

"But that's silly. Such a little thing."

"You have yet to learn about artistic temperament, Abigail. Actors throw tantrums, knock their heads against walls, and go into hysterics over the tiniest imagined slight. They're not adults, you know, simply big kids."

Without removing his eyes from the road, Forsythe said, "It seems to me I've heard that expression used about writers too."

"Not this one. I haven't a touch of temperament. Fully adult, worst luck. But if you don't believe me, wait and see."

They didn't have long to wait. Forsythe piloted the Rover into a coach house now used as a garage and found the Ferrari was already in its place. Dowling was lovingly rubbing down its blazing flanks as one might groom a favorite mare. Erika, cradling the sheaf of orchids in her arms, stood close to him. Without looking up from his work Dowling was issuing orders. "Grab a rag; that's a good girl; get to work on the hubcaps."

The girl looked around for a place to deposit her flowers and Giles picked up a clean cloth and bent to the hubcaps. Dowling raised his brows. "Not like you to be helpful. What's got into you?"

"Probably the only chance I'll ever have for contact with your scarlet beast. Think rainwater is going to dissolve it?"

The actor transferred his attention and a dry cloth to the grill. "Ever hear of rust? Trouble with most people is they buy something and then neglect it. Know what I paid for this car?"

Nobody showed any interest in the price, but Dowling proceeded to tell them anyway. He'd worked into the price of leather seats when the ancient Bentley puffed its way into the garage and Marcia erupted from the passenger seat. She stood with her legs straddled, glaring at the exotic blooms glowing against Erika's anorak. Glancing up apprehensively, Giles made a move to get between the two women but he was too late. Marcia spat, "You bitch! You've got everything else, might as well have these!" She threw her violets at the girl, hitting her under one eye, burst into a storm of tears, and lunged out of the door.

Erika called after her and Dowling, without glancing away from a fender, laughed. "She used the right word anyway. If there ever was a green-eyed bitch, it's Marcia Mather. Pay no attention, Erika, she's doing the woman-scorned act."

Erika looked as though she were on the verge of tears and her aunt went to her and took the orchids. "I'll put these in your room, dear." Stooping, she retrieved the nosegay of violets. "They're a bit bruised but Potty loves violets. I'll give them to her."

"Perhaps if you give the orchids to Marcia, Aunt Honoria, she'll feel better."

"I think not. Probably incense her even more."

Borthwick and Cochrane were now out of the Bentley and the director said, "We'd better get in, Sam, and see if we can smooth her ruffled feathers down."

Huge shoulders moved in a shrug. "I suppose we can give it a try."

Cochrane didn't sound hopeful but he did follow Borthwick. Forsythe touched his secretary's arm and jerked his head. As they trotted through the rain Giles Eady caught up with them. Ignoring him, Miss Sanderson said contritely to Forsythe, "I'm sorry I got you into this, Robby."

Giles put a comradely arm around her damp shoulders. "Not to worry. By dinner time all will be sweetness and light."

This time the writer was mistaken. Dinner proved to be an uncomfortable meal. Despite excellent food, candlelight, and wine, most of the faces around the oval table were glum. Not only was Marcia's shapely nose red but so were her eyelids. She didn't say a word, not even to Honoria. As usual Cochrane was taciturn and the generally talkative Borthwick spoke only once, to ask for salt to be passed. Michael Dowling, at Honoria's right paid little attention to his hostess. He talked incessantly, mainly about housing estates and how foolish Leslie Koster was to hold on to his farm.

"I happen to agree with the boy," Honoria told him. "Kosters have lived on that farm as long as Farqusons have lived here. Money would be a poor substitute."

"Let me tell you about money," Dowling said. "I grew up on a dirt farm in the Midwest and . . ."

Forsythe stopped listening. This he'd heard before. He was heartily sick of the entire business and was relieved when dinner was finally over and a general exodus began.

Coffee and brandy were being served in the drawing room but Giles went in the direction of the library. Honoria was trying to interest her remaining guests in a table of bridge. Miss Sanderson, Borthwick, and Cochrane were persuaded and Potter brought in a card table and proceeded to set it up.

The barrister had every intention of going to his room and escaping into the pages of a book, but Dowling followed him into the hall. "How about a game of billiards, Robert?"

"Can I play too?" Erika asked.

"You can watch. You're a lousy player but I've a hunch Robert may be pretty good."

Forsythe *was* good so he grimly decided he would play. Do no harm to take this conceited ass down a peg or two. The three of them went into the billiard room, located at the back of the house near the kitchen, and proceeded to play. To Forsythe's chagrin he found that Dowling, although he made unnecessary flourishes, was a splendid player, far out of the barrister's league. Erika proved impartial, applauding every good shot regardless of by whom it was made. Forsythe did his best but he knew what the outcome would be. Finally Dowling struck a pose and, with a flourish, made a brilliant bank shot. He stood back and grinned at the barrister. "That's it. Licked you. You're not bad, Robert, but out of your class."

Muttering a silent curse, Forsythe racked his cue. It was then he noticed the silent figure leaning against the doorjamb. Marcia had changed into a caftan of a rich ruby velvet. Makeup was applied with a lavish hand and she'd managed to almost hide the redness around her nostrils. He could catch the scent of strong perfume from where he stood. From behind him, Dowling asked sarcastically, "Decided to stop sulking, old girl? Care to have a game?"

"I don't play games. I'd like to have that overdue chat."

"Talk away."

She jerked her head. "Upstairs, Mickey Darling."

He was chalking his cue. "Anything you want to say, you'll have to say right here."

"I don't think you'd care for that."

At her tone he glanced up. "Why the change? You're looking like a pussy full of cream."

She took his arm. "Come along, Mickey."

For a moment he seemed indecisive, then he shrugged. "Don't go away, Robert. I'll be back shortly for a rematch."

Erika was staring after them. "What is she up to now?" Turning her head she told Forsythe ingenuously, "Marcia doesn't like me."

"I rather gathered that. Would you care for a game while we're waiting?"

"I'm not good at it. I've played a few times with Mickey but he's such a wonderful player he makes me nervous. But I would like to try, Robert."

Forsythe set the table up and allowed the girl to take the first shot. He felt suddenly content and at peace. The quiet of the room was broken only by the thud of cue against ball, the rustle of Erika's long cotton skirt as she moved around the table. He paid little attention to his own game, content to watch the girl, the grace of her wrists as she handled the cue, the soft fall of her hair against her face, the shadows cast by lashes on high cheekbones. As she bent and straightened he could smell her odor, a perfume entirely different from Marcia Mather's, this one the innocent fragrance of growing things. This exquisite creature, he thought dismally, is soon going to be the wife of Mickey Darling.

He wondered whether Dowling did have any affection for her. Whether he'd been misjudged and did actually love the girl. Hopefully Forsythe considered the expression on the actor's face when Giles Eady had claimed his kiss, the fury

76

and the anger. Perhaps . . . then Forsythe shook his head. He remembered a week he'd spent at a client's house in Kent. The client, an aging man named Smythe, had a consuming passion, the collection of antique lusterware. It was kept behind locked doors, in glass cases lining the walls. As a special favor he'd unlocked the doors and while Smythe proudly showed the barrister the objects in the cases, another guest, this a rather brash young man, wandered to a small table in the center of the room where the prize of the collection was standing under a glass dome. Lifting the dome, he picked up the tiny vase and was turning it in his hands. Smythe turned his head, saw what was going on, broke into a howling rage, and ordered the young man from the house. Smythe's expression had been exactly that of Dowling's when Giles had kissed his fiancée. So, Forsythe admitted, Erika was only another possession, the star of his collection. After Dowling drained her dry, took everything he could get, she'd doubtless join the other discarded young women in his past.

A tide of rage swept over the barrister. He could understand how Borthwick, Cochrane, and Giles felt. Magic was rare and should be protected and cherished.

Erika's voice broke into his reverie. "I asked if you were letting me win, Robert."

Forsythe opened his mouth to deny this and then to his horror heard himself quoting from Euphues. " 'So beautie allureth the chast minds to love, and the wisest witte to lust.' "

The girl was looking at him without comprehension and Forsythe didn't blame her. A dignified barrister, he thought, a man nearing middle years, bleating quotations like a lovesick calf!

"I don't—" Erika started to say.

"Mr. Forsythe!"

He spun around. Honoria stood in the doorway, a hand

clasped to her breast. "Come quickly! Mickey is shouting down the stairs. About Marcia. She must be hurt or ill."

Forsythe dropped his cue and ran past her. A group of people were standing at the foot of the stairs, their faces turned upward. On the landing Dowling was leaning against the bannister for support. "Don't any of you understand? She's having a fit of some kind!"

Forsythe took the stairs two at a time with Miss Sanderson at his heels. Wordlessly Dowling pointed down the hall. A door stood open spilling light across the carpet. Forsythe pulled to a halt. In the middle of the bedroom was a round table covered with a lace cloth. On it sat a tray with a partially full bottle of whiskey and an unopened bottle of mineral water. Beside the tray a crystal glass lay on its side, amber liquid draining from it, puddling on the lace. A chair was lying on its side and near it, on the Turkish carpet, sprawled a figure in ruby velvet.

Miss Sanderson grabbed at his arm. "Watch the glass."

He circled around the splinters of glass and knelt. Marcia lay on her back. The caftan was twisted and hiked up over her long white legs. The skin of her face was mottled and empty eyes stared sightlessly at the ceiling. The horror was her mouth. Painted lips drew back from her teeth in a dreadful rictus, as though she were silently screaming. Forsythe's hands moved over her throat, over her wrists. He sniffed at her lips and then looked up at his secretary. "Keep them out, Sandy."

Miss Sanderson stretched out long arms, barring the doorway. From somewhere behind her, Honoria called, "I rang through to Doctor Blake's home but he's out on an emergency. Shall I—"

"No rush now, Miss Farquson." With difficulty Forsythe pulled himself up. He'd forgotten about his bad leg but it was making its presence known. "She's dead."

78

"What is it?" Borthwick demanded. "Heart attack, stroke?"

Dowling's handsome face poked over Miss Sanderson's shoulder. "She had a fit! When I got back from the bathroom with the glass she was jerking all over the floor." He added as though it mattered greatly, "I dropped the glass and it broke."

Forsythe limped toward the door. "Sandy, go down and ring the police. The rest of you get out of here. I'm shutting this room up until they get here."

"Why? This is my room. I've got a perfect right—" Dowling broke off and the color drained from his face. The glowing bronze skin turned suddenly muddy. "What happened to her?"

"She's been poisoned."

Dowling let out a howl, not a shout, more a scream. He jerked Miss Sanderson's arm down and stepped in front of her. One sandal came squarely down on a shard of glass but he didn't seem to know it.

"She had a drink of *my* whiskey." He looked wildly around. "Don't you understand? *My* whiskey. Someone tried to kill *me*."

Then, incredibly, he broke into a high-pitched laugh, a laugh of pure hysteria.

Pushing the man from the room, Forsythe closed the door on his laughing face.

CHAPTER SEVEN

Forsythe woke slowly and with reluctance, feeling hardly up to the effort of opening his eyes. In the dim light his secretary's face hovered above him. Sandy looked as exhausted as he felt. Violet shadows encircled her eyes and her skin was ashen. Removing her hand from his shoulder, she pulled back the curtains and brilliant sunlight dazzled him.

He struggled up against the pillows. "Fine day."

"As far as weather is concerned, yes."

"What time is it? I feel as though I'd only just put my head down."

"After eleven. You can't have been in bed long. I didn't get to my room until four and you were still down with Chief Inspector Parker. I hated to waken you but your presence is urgently requested."

Pushing his legs over the side of the bed, he reached for his robe. "I rather thought Chief Inspector Parker had drained me dry last night, or I guess I should say this morning."

"Reinforcements have arrived from London."

"Parker didn't waste any time yelling for help. Anyone we know?"

"Chief Inspector Adam Kepesake and his man Friday, Detective Sergeant Brummell."

Forsythe stretched and looked at the napkin-covered tray. "Breakfast?"

"Coffee and rolls. The best I could do. Things are a bit hectic in the servant's quarters."

Forsythe sat down and poured coffee. "Potter and his wife seem unflappable."

"They are and the older maid, Sarah, is taking her cue from them but her sister Edie is in a dreadful state."

"How are our hostess and the other guests?"

"Honoria is in bad shape. I insisted she remain in bed this morning. Erika's hands are full with her fiancé. They're barricaded in the late colonel's bedroom and a password is needed to enter. Mickey Darling certainly made a spectacle of himself last night. As soon as you shut the door he proceeded to go into raving hysterics. Most of us just stood around embarrassed and helpless but Cochrane came to the rescue and batted the golden boy right across the face. After that Erika led him away sobbing."

Forsythe spread marmalade lavishly on a roll. "*That* I wish I could have seen. So the dynamic duo are with us. How are Kepesake and Beau Brummell?"

"The chief inspector still resembles a male model and as usual poor Beau looks as if he'd slept in his clothes. What an unlikely nickname for such a slovenly man."

"With that surname I suppose it was inevitable. But we could have drawn worse officers. Kepesake and Brummell are bright and competent. Are you and I on the list of suspects?"

"No. I had the impression the chief inspector was a bit disappointed about that. But seeing we only met this group of people a couple of days ago it's a little difficult to uncover a motive." Miss Sanderson perched on the foot of the bed. She looked disconsolate and her next remark bore that out. "To think, Robby, I was responsible for pushing this vacation. Right now I wish I was back in our chambers and my peaceful flat was waiting."

Draining his cup, he stood up. "Can't turn back the clock, Sandy. Have they decided the type of poison and its source?"

"You were bang on. Cyanide, and quite possibly from Leslie Koster's little lab."

"That's what I thought. The crystals, once they hit liquid, have quite a distinct odor and I remembered seeing a bottle boldly labeled 'cyanide' on Koster's shelf. Now, you'd better get out of here, Sandy. I have to shave and dress. Maybe I'll feel human when I do. Tell the gendarmes I'll be with them in half an hour."

"Better make it sooner. The chief inspector is champing at the bit."

When Forsythe arrived at the colonel's library he found Chief Inspector Kepesake looking impatient. The air was blue with smoke and Kepesake was inserting another cigarette into his jade holder. Miss Sanderson's assessment of his looks was dead accurate. He was a model of sartorial elegance and his hair looked as though he'd had it freshly styled. The hazel eyes were as deceptively kind as ever.

"Ah, Forsythe, come in. Do be seated. You have a habit of turning up, don't you?"

Forsythe took the chair across the desk from the chief inspector. "Do I detect the words 'like a bad penny' tickling your tongue?"

"Definitely not. I'm delighted you're here. Nothing like having a skilled observer. Now, you met Chief Inspector Parker of the County Constabulary last night." Forsythe nodded at Parker. He looked youthful for his rank, a trim young man with a pink boyish face. As though to counteract that look of dewy youth, Parker had cultivated a fledgling mustache that succeeded in making him look still younger. The jade holder moved. "Of course you know Sergeant Brummell and this is Police Constable Summer of the County Constabulary. Summer, open a window a crack; the smoke is making my eyes water." Kepesake's gold lighter flickered and he lit his cigarette.

Forsythe contemplated the remark about a skilled observer. Kepesake was not in the habit of buttering him up. "I don't know how I can be of assistance." He nodded at the stack of files on the desk in front of Parker. "I told Chief Inspector Parker all I know last night."

"Fully and concisely, and I appreciate it. But I must admit I seem to be out of my depth. I've never dealt with theatrical people before and, reading over those statements, I find I'm confused. And artistic temperaments! Mr. Dowling flatly refuses to come down for an interview. Sent a message if I wanted to see him I could damn well go up to him."

Forsythe grinned. "Probably terrified he'll be attacked on the stairs by an ax-wielding maniac. What do you find puzzling about the statements?"

"The way these people babble on and on. Volunteering every detail. With the exception of—what's his name?"

"Cochrane," Chief Inspector Parker said. "Samuel Cochrane. He's the head of the camera section and supposed to be top-notch in his profession. It was like pulling teeth to get anything out of him. All the rest told me their life histories. Made no bones about either hating Michael Dowling or, in Miss Farr's case, of adoring him."

"Yes, they do speak freely," Forsythe agreed, thinking of Dowling's confidences the afternoon he'd arrived. "But you must remember they're not like people in other professions. Their entire lives revolve around drama."

Kepesake removed the butt from his holder, snubbed it

out, and inserted a fresh cigarette. "You realize what we have here, Forsythe? With the exception of you and Miss Sanderson we have an entire household with the opportunity and the motives to want Michael Dowling dead. I've drawn up a list of people above suspicion. You and Miss Sanderson head it and other than you there are only two names. The maids—Sarah and Edith Perkins."

Parker was fingering his fledgling mustache. "I think Miss Farquson's name should be included on that list. I grew up in Bury-Sutton and I've known her all my life. She's a gentle old-fashioned lady."

"Gentle ladies have been known to murder before," Kepesake told him dryly.

"Not Miss Farquson. If there was an ounce of violence in her I tell you where it would have come out. She'd have murdered her father. If there ever was a candidate for a bloody murder it was that devil."

Kepesake shook his head. "Miss Farquson stays as a suspect. She had opportunity and a good motive."

Forsythe was loading his pipe. Might as well add to the smoky atmosphere. "Are you convinced *Dowling* was the target?"

"Not convinced but it doesn't seem likely the poison was meant for Miss Mather." Leaning over the desk, Kepesake tapped the file folders neatly arranged before his colleague. "In every one of these statements, including the butler's and cook's, it's evident the speaker was aware of Dowling's . . . ah, peculiarity in regard to his personal possessions. Mr. Eady states that 'Mickey Darling wouldn't give a man dying of thirst a drink from his water bottle.' Mr. Borthwick says that in all the years he has known Mr. Dowling he never offered a drink. Apparently the only person he ever shows generosity to is his fiancée, Miss Farr—"

"Erika," Forsythe stiffened. "Could the poison have been planned not only for Dowling but for Erika?"

"That thought occurred to me," Parker said. "But, again, all of them are aware that Miss Farr never touched whiskey. She hates it. All she drinks is wine and an occasional martini."

Kepesake nodded his head. "I can't see a murderer trying to kill either Miss Farr or Miss Mather by putting cyanide in Dowling's whiskey bottle. Referring again to the statements, no one was aware Miss Mather was in Mr. Dowling's room last evening. They claim they never went upstairs after dinner. Is that right, Forsythe?"

"Miss Farr and Dowling and I were in the billiard room. Miss Mather came to see us there, demanded that Dowling speak with her, and they left. Miss Farr and I were together until Miss Farquson came to sound the alarm. I can't tell you about the others."

"Miss Sanderson vouched for the bridge players. Said Mr. Cochrane, Mr. Borthwick, and Miss Farquson didn't leave the drawing room until they heard Dowling calling down the stairs. Mr. Eady says he was here in the library working."

Sergeant Brummell spoke for the first time. "Miss Mather might have told someone earlier that she was going to talk to Dowling last evening."

His superior swung around. "How would they know it would be in Dowling's room? It could have been anywhere in the house."

With a big hand Brummell rumpled his already untidy hair. "Miss Mather hated Dowling. Maybe she poisoned herself trying to get him convicted of her murder."

Kepesake turned back to the barrister. "You must have received some impression about the woman's character. What do you think, Forsythe?"

"She wasn't the type. Marcia Mather was vindictive and I believe would have gone to many lengths to avenge herself on Michael Dowling but . . . no, I can't see her sacrificing her own life."

Parker frowned. "If Miss Mather was the target only one person could have killed her. Michael Dowling."

Leaning back in his chair, Kepesake blew a perfect smoke ring, regarded it, and muttered. "That would have been an incredibly stupid move. Dowling would be the only suspect. Forsythe, is he a stupid man?"

Forsythe took his time answering. Chief Inspector Kepesake seemed to regard him as an expert on the film people. He put his thoughts into words. "I've only known these people for about forty-eight hours. Hardly long enough to be an expert on their characters. I was told that Dowling is quite shrewd; the actual words were 'he has a type of low cunning.' My impression of him, for what it's worth, is that although he's vain and arrogant and totally insensitive he's not stupid. He strikes me as a person who values his own hide."

Parker laughed and even his laugh was boyish. "Reminds me of what that writer, Eady, said to the same question. 'Mickey Darling,' he said, 'would have slipped the poison in Marcia's glass, not the bottle. Wouldn't catch the golden boy ruining a bottle of good liquor.' The way these people talk!"

His colleague from the Central Bureau didn't seem to care for Parker's lightheartedness. Giving him an admonishing glance, Kepesake said sternly, "No matter how colorful they are, there's a murderer among them. But how to pick him or her out? That director, Borthwick, raved on about Dowling being responsible for his wife's suicide. Giles Eady admitted he hates Dowling's guts, fights with him constantly, has been in love with Miss Farr since he met her years ago—"

"I like the words he used," Parker broke in. Apparently his colleague's reprimand hadn't quenched him and he wore a broad smile. "He said Miss Farr 'couldn't even see him' and it had been 'love at first slight.' "

This time Kepesake didn't spare a glance in Parker's direction. "Take Samuel Cochrane—Forsythe, have you heard about his daughter?"

"A little. Not specific details."

"A sordid and horrible business. Cochrane admitted he'd heard rumors that Dowling was the man responsible and it wouldn't surprise me if there was a connection there. This is in strictest confidence, Forsythe, but narcotics division have had their eyes on Dowling for months. Seems they had an anonymous tip that the actor was smuggling drugs into the country—"

"A user?" Forsythe interrupted.

"A dealer. The tipster said he's supplying hard drugs to members of the theatrical community. Narcotics division haven't been able to catch him at it. But to get back to Cochrane's daughter . . . Parker, perhaps you'd better fill Forsythe in."

Parker was now as serious as Kepesake. "Had to drag the information out of the poor chap. According to him his daughter Jenny was a good girl, never gave a bit of trouble. Her mother died when the child was four and Cochrane raised her with Jenny's godmother's help. Said he blames himself and Marcia Mather—"

"Marcia?" Forsythe blurted.

It was Kepesake's turn to smile broadly. "Ah! I see our sleuth didn't ferret that tidbit out. Shame on you, Forsythe! Yes, Marcia Mather was the girl's godmother. Carry on, Parker."

"Cochrane says he and Miss Mather were too busy to keep a proper eye on the girl. Jenny was left in the care of a housekeeper. The same old story. The girl pretended she was staying overnight at friends' houses and sneaked out on the sly to meet a man. He hooked her on drugs and got her with child. Four months ago the girl locked herself into her bedroom and took an overdose. At that time Miss Mather was on the Continent and Cochrane was in the States. Rumors reached Cochrane about Dowling, but he said there was no proof the actor was the monster who had done it."

For a time they sat quietly, the silence broken only by the tick of a mantel clock and the rustling as Parker leafed through a folder labeled with Samuel Cochrane's name. The constable stood practically at attention near the window; Brummell slouched with an elbow on the mantel, seeming to study the tips of his unpolished shoes; Kepesake was gazing off into space. Forsythe gazed past Brummell's shoulder at Colonel Farquson's narrow dark face. He fancied there was a gleam of sardonic amusement in the painted eyes.

Parker broke the silence. He cleared his throat. "I asked each of the men the same question—were they responsible for the attempt on Dowling's life. Here their answers are, Mr. Forsythe." Pages flipped over. "Cochrane—a blunt 'No.' I asked him what he would have done if he'd had proof Dowling was the man responsible for his daughter's suicide. Answer—'I wouldn't have poisoned him. I'd have torn him apart with my bare hands.' Melvin Borthwick spoke at some length. He said at the time of his wife's death he went looking for Michael Dowling with a revolver and if he could have found the man he'd have shot him." Parker glanced up at the barrister. "Damning statement, isn't it? But then he said Mrs. Borthwick died four years ago and Dowling had sense enough to keep clear until he— Borthwick—had cooled down. Borthwick stated that he would never forgive Dowling but he had long realized nothing could bring back his wife and his children—he has three—have lost their mother and he can't deprive them of a father. Borthwick also said, and I quote, 'Four years is a long time to keep rage at a fever pitch. I'm not that type of man. I flare up and then simmer down. I also realize Beth was an adult and no one forced her to run after her lover. No, I did not try to poison Michael Dowling.'"

"Giles Eady?" Forsythe asked.

Parker flipped open another file and his lips twitched. "'I assure you I'm sorry poor Marcia was killed in Mickey Darling's stead. I also assure you if I'd made the attempt I wouldn't have gotten an innocent bystander. And, no, I did not try to poison the golden boy.'"

Tapping his pipe dottle out in a glass ashtray, Forsythe spoke to Chief Inspector Kepesake. "That list of the people you don't suspect . . . I notice Erika Von Farr's name isn't included."

"I haven't interviewed her yet. The only people I've had time to see are Miss Sanderson, briefly, and now you. But I've read over the information Parker got last night and yes, Miss Farr is still among the suspects. She had the same opportunity as the others to obtain and use the cyanide. Correct me if I'm wrong but any one of you could have slipped into Koster's laboratory and taken the cyanide. After you returned from your visit to the greenhouse any of you could have gone into Dowling's bedroom and put the poison in the whiskey bottle."

Forsythe closed his eyes, his mind running over the events of the previous day. "We didn't stay in a group at the greenhouse. All of us wandered around engrossed in the plants. It's not one large room, you know. It's a series of rooms. It would have been simple to get the cyanide without being observed and there the bottle was on the shelf, clearly labeled—"

"Leslie Koster's eyesight is poor," Parker broke in. "At school we called him 'the mole.'"

Forsythe's eyes snapped open. "What does Koster use cyanide for?"

"Fertilizer," Parker told him. "Koster gave me a long

89

lecture on every type he makes up. Seems he uses—" he flipped through a notebook this time— "a combination of lime and carbon as well as other names I can't even pronounce. He's never worried about having the poison sitting on a shelf. He handles the mixing himself and says few people except staff are ever allowed in the greenhouse. Koster was reluctant to admit the poison could be his but did say the level seemed lower in the bottle than it was the last time he'd used it."

"Then he has no idea how much is missing?" Forsythe asked.

"None. All we know is there was enough poison in that whiskey bottle to finish off the entire household."

Forsythe focused his attention on Kepesake. "Very well. The poison was accessible to any one of us. Again, any one of us could have gone into Dowling's room before dinner. Let's get back to Erika Von Farr. Certainly she had the opportunity and could have gotten the means, but what motive could she have to want Dowling dead?"

"Haven't discovered any yet but I'm keeping an open mind."

"And Miss Farquson?"

"A good motive. She admitted Miss Mather had filled her in on Dowling's lurid past. Do you think she wants to see her niece, the only relative she has left, marrying a man like that?"

"Miss Farquson also stated that she didn't believe a word that Miss Mather said," Parker said stiffly. "She said Miss Mather obviously had a grudge against the actor and was trying to make trouble. Miss Farquson has also given her blessing to her niece and Dowling and is going to deed over this estate to them when they marry."

"That's what she *said*," Kepesake pointed out.

"Miss Farquson's word is inviolate. And what about the

Potters? How can you possibly suspect those old people?" Parker demanded.

"It wouldn't take much strength to open a bottle and pour cyanide into it."

"How did they get the poison? They weren't at the greenhouse. And just what would be the motive? They're a fine old couple. I've known them all—"

"—your life," Kepesake finished for him. "I'm afraid, Chief Inspector Parker, you're allowing personal relationships to cloud your professional judgment. Miss Farquson could have given them the poison and from what you've told me about those old servants they'd cut off their arms for their mistress." The local inspector subsided grumbling and Kepesake appealed to Forsythe. "Now, you've got most of what we know. For God sake's clarify the picture for me."

"In what way?"

The chief inspector's hand moved along his hair as though he was tempted to run his fingers through it and then dropped away from its perfection. "These theatrical people, I can't make head or tail of them. Here we have three of them, four counting the dead woman, who have good reasons for loathing the ground Dowling walks on. And what do they do? Work closely with him. Spend a weekend cooped up in this house with a man who was responsible for one woman's suicide, and suspected of the horrible death of a girl little more than a child. Why?"

Before Forsythe could answer, Parker, who appeared to have his second wind, said slyly, "Giles Eady answered that already."

"I read it. 'Show biz.' Spare me any more of that man's pithy comments."

"Eady made sense. Said in the film business if you worked only with people you liked you wouldn't be working."

A brick-like color was sweeping across Kepesake's face

and the hazel eyes no longer looked kind. Forsythe hastened to intervene. "Perhaps I can help there. I understand all of them, except Miss Mather, are involved emotionally as well as professionally with Miss Farr. They're working on this film because of her and are hoping to talk her out of appearing with Michael Dowling. Now, it might be helpful if you could fill me in on Dowling's description of his talk with Miss Mather."

Kepesake jerked his head at the younger inspector and turned his attention to another cigarette. The constable coughed and opened the window wider. Parker flipped through his papers and selected one. "Dowling wouldn't come downstairs last night. I had to go up to the room he'd locked himself into and Miss Farr was with him. Dowling refused to let her leave so I took both their statements there. He said when Miss Mather and he went upstairs they turned into his bedroom. Miss Mather's room was farther down the hall near the bathroom and they just automatically turned into his. They sat down at the table and Miss Mather proceeded to beg him for a larger part in the film, told him her career was in jeopardy and a larger role would make it easier to get other jobs. Dowling turned her down flat. He said the actress then became abusive, throwing up things from their past, claiming he had ruined her. To quiet her down he suggested they have a drink. As he had only one glass in his room he left her and went down to the bathroom, where he'd noticed a row of glasses on a shelf. The glass looked a bit dusty and so he took a moment to rinse it out. When he got back to his room he found Miss Mather hadn't waited. She'd poured whiskey in the glass and it was tipped over with its contents all over the table. Miss Mather was on the floor, jerking and twitching around. Dowling said he didn't dream of poison; he thought she was having a fit of some kind. He ran to the top of the stairs and called down for help."

Up to this point the young policeman had been brisk and businesslike. Now he grinned and said with relish, "My wife is a Mickey Darling fan. Drags me to every picture he's made. I wish she could have seen him last night. A bowl of jelly!"

Kepesake grimaced. "Mr. Dowling is coming down here to *me*. No way I'm going up to him. Well, you know all we do now, Forsythe. Any ideas?"

"You had one piece of information I didn't. I had no idea Miss Mather was Jenny Cochrane's godmother." Forsythe got up. His leg had stiffened up again.

"One moment. We do have another piece of information. I wasn't going to give it to you but—" He swiveled around. "What do you think, Beau?"

"I'd give it, sir. Mr. Forsythe's close as a clam."

"And we have reason to know that only too well, don't we? Very well. Before the County Constabulary arrived last evening, Miss Mather's room was given a hasty search."

Forsythe sat down again. "Are you certain?"

"The upstairs maid was. Beau and I took her into the room this morning shortly after we got down here. Her younger sister, Edith, is a mess. So scared she can hardly talk, but this older sister is a levelheaded woman. Sarah Perkins took one look and said someone had been rummaging around in the dead woman's room. Sarah said Miss Mather was meticulous, and when we entered the room the bottom drawer in the chest was ajar, with a sweater hanging out of it. The top drawer, where the woman kept her hankies and scarves, was a jumble. Sarah swore they were always perfectly piled, the edged aligned. Not only that but the bedspread had been hiked up and the lower sheet pulled out as though the mattress had been lifted. Sarah said she'd been in Miss Mather's room to turn down the bed during the dinner hour and all was in order at that time."

"Hmm." Forsythe gazed at the colonel's portrait without

93

seeing it. "A small item. Nothing of any size could be hidden under a pile of hankies or scarves. You said before the county police arrived. Are you certain?"

"As soon as we got here Summer went to Miss Mather's room and locked it." It was Parker's turn to swivel toward his constable. "Isn't that right, Summer?"

"That's correct, sir. The butler gave me the key from a ring; seems there's only one key per room and they generally aren't used. I went directly to the victim's room and locked the door. Kept the key right here—" he patted the breast pocket on his tunic— "till Chief Inspector Kepesake arrived. Gave it into his hands, sir."

"In that case," Forsythe mused, "the search must have taken place after Marcia Mather's death. Between dinner time and the time of her death only Marcia Mather and Dowling were on the first floor. I closed myself into Dowling's room with the body and Sandy joined me as soon as she'd rung through the police. Let me see . . . the body was discovered at about eleven. Chief Inspector Parker and his constables arrived at—"

"Eleven thirty-seven, Mr. Forsythe," Parker told him. "We had to drive from Elleston. I know what you're going to ask. Which person could have gone to Miss Mather's room and searched it in that time span? The answer is everyone in the house."

"Not again?" Forsythe asked.

Parker's notebook snapped open again. "I've made a list of movements. After you closed yourself in the murder room the three men—Borthwick, Eady, Cochrane—came downstairs in a group. Eady offered the others a drink of brandy in this room." His eyes lifted and he pointed to a tray with an assortment of glasses and a decanter. "Cochrane declined and headed for the front door. When we got here he was pacing up and down the driveway in front of the house, soaked to the skin from the downpour. Borthwick went along with Eady. He gulped down a brandy and left Eady alone here. Says he went into the drawing room, built up the fire, and he was there when we arrived."

"Erika Von Farr?" the barrister asked.

The younger chief inspector said, "Had to take Dowling in hand. There was an unpleasantness after you closed them out in the hall and Dowling got completely out of hand. Cochrane slapped his face and Dowling broke down and started to cry." Looking rather pleased, Parker continued, "Miss Farr told her aunt she was taking Dowling to her own room, but Miss Farquson's a very proper lady and wouldn't hear of it. Ended up with Miss Farquson ordering her niece to take him to the only bedroom not in use, one that had been her father's, so they went to it. Dowling wanted to lock the door and there wasn't a key, so Miss Farr went downstairs, found the kitchen in an uproar with her aunt trying to quiet down Edith Perkins, and finally got the key from the butler. She went back to the colonel's room and it took some time to get in. Dowling had piled furniture in front of the door. The two of them spent the rest of the time there."

Parker paused to catch his breath and Forsythe prompted, "Miss Farquson?"

"She went downstairs and found Potter looking for her. Edith Perkins was in an awful state, figured she was going to be murdered at any minute, so Miss Farquson went to the kitchen, where Sarah and Mrs. Potter were trying to calm the girl. Miss Farquson managed to quiet Edith a bit, got some tea in her, and then decided to go to the morning room. Miss Farquson said she needed time to compose herself. The Potters were all over the house. So, Mr. Forsythe, any of the people here could have made a hasty search of Miss Mather's room."

"Borthwick was in the drawing room," Forsythe pointed out. "Anyone using the stairs would have been spotted by him."

"The doors were shut. Borthwick said he wanted privacy."

This time Kepesake did run his fingers through his hair. "Damnedest thing I've ever seen. Like shadow boxing. Why couldn't you have kept an eye on these people until Parker got here, Forsythe?"

"Rather difficult to be in two places at one time. And I thought it was best to remain at the scene of the crime." He regarded Kepesake warily, "Why are you baring your breast like this?"

"As I said, I need any help I can get. The media is bombarding the gates. I have constables down there fending them off. Television crews, reporters, radio outfits . . . my neck is on the line. Going to be pressure from all directions."

"I have never," Forsythe said bluntly, "thought you had a high opinion of me."

"You're wrong." Kepesake flipped up a hand. "Tell him, Beau."

Sergeant Brummell flopped into a chair beside the barrister's. "The chief and I admire you. Sure, we've had our differences but take that case of the moor murders last year. If you hadn't spotted that those three schoolgirls weren't wearing undershirts, we'd never have caught up with their killer. I guess you've been lucky but you got an eye for little things, things nobody pays any mind to. That's what the chief is trying to tell you."

"Well said, Beau!" For a moment Forsythe thought Kepesake was going to applaud. "Little things, that's your forte. You and Miss Sanderson make quite a team. And you're right on the spot. Perhaps you'll notice something or maybe you already have and—"

"I don't suppose you'd consider letting Sandy or me leave. We're not on your suspect list."

Pulling himself up, Kepesake stretched. "You're both staying right here."

"One hell of a place to spend a vacation."

"Let's put it this way, Forsythe. The sooner this case is cracked, the sooner you can get on with your vacation. Now, get to work and spot those tiny details."

"It will be impossible to keep us here after the inquest."

"Ah, but when will that be?"

Indeed, Forsythe thought, when will the inquest be? It looked as though Chief Inspector Kepesake was determined to get as much help as he could from a lowly barrister and his secretary.

In the hall outside the library two people were waiting. One was Samuel Cochrane, who had time only to nod before Constable Summer ushered him into the room. The other was Miss Sanderson, an apron tied around her narrow waist and a feather duster clutched in one hand. She raised her brows and Forsythe told her, "Borders on police brutality. The chief inspector is intent on keeping us around. Feels out of his depth with this crowd and wants us to act as spies."

"Nothing but cheap blackmail!"

"Precisely. I'm feeling a trifle peckish. Is lunch laid on?"

"A buffet in the morning room, but I was thinking of packing a basket and we'll eat outside. There's a summer house at the foot of the garden."

"Fine idea. The walls do tend to close in. I'll wait for you there."

The barrister wandered out the front door, through the portico, and down the winding driveway. He reached the final curve and from there could see three stalwart constables, aided by Heathcliff, guarding the gates. Retreating, he strolled across rich turf toward the garden. Sunshine beamed warmly down, blossoms wafted their scent, and with the Georgian house well behind him, he began to feel more cheerful.

CHAPTER EIGHT

AFTER A TIME, FORSYTHE FOUND HE'D LOST HIS BEAR-
ings. Directly ahead was a low hedge and as he drew level
with it he spotted a kitchen garden. Near the hedge the full
black moon of an ample behind was poised over a row of
radishes. He cleared his throat and the black moon rose in
stately motion until it assumed the proportions of a
lookalike for the royal Victoria. Mrs. Potter, even with her
skirt hiked up and a scarf hiding her topknot, bore an
uncanny resemblance to that lady. She also wore an
expression indicating that she too was not amused.

"Looking for something?" she rasped.

"The summer house."

"Go back to those lime trees. Follow them. An idiot
couldn't miss it."

Forsythe thought of Adam Kepesake and decided he
might as well get to work. He offered a small olive branch.
"Nice garden."

"Should be. Miss Honoria works her fingers to the bone
on it." Mrs. Potter bent to her work.

Digging his pipe from his pocket, Forsythe proceeded to load it. "You've been on the estate a long time."

"Over half a century. Potter and me came before Miss Honoria was born." The cook critically examined a radish and then dropped it into her basket. "Never had a child of our own."

An oblique way, Forsythe thought, of letting me know they regard Honoria as a daughter and are not about to gossip about her. He tried another tack. "Seem to be a lot of locals milling around by the gates."

"No doubt having the time of their lives." Mrs. Potter snorted and hoisted herself up with less dignity than the first time. "Telling everything they know and a sight they don't to get their pictures in the papers or see themselves on telly. All I can say is they got mighty short memories. Miss Honoria's done a lot for them. Just last winter spent money for her own coat on one for the Widow Clement. Told her she was a fool but she says she can stand the cold better than the old lady. Lot of thanks she'll be getting!"

Encouraged by this long speech, Forsythe sent out a feeler. "I suppose you knew Miss Mather when she was a child."

"Didn't take to her then and felt the same when she come down here last week. Naughty, sneaking brat Marcy Mather was. Always thinking up mischief and then laying it on Terry Sanderson or Miss Honoria." The withered lips seemed to be trembling on the verge of "good riddance," but then they firmed. She contented herself with saying, "Never came near Miss Honoria all these years. Must admit Miss Teresa did some better. Didn't mind her but liked her sister a sight better. Miss Sanderson dug in and helped this morning. Kept Miss Honoria in bed where she ought to be too."

Cupping his hands, Forsythe managed to get his pipe going. "Miss Mather didn't seem to like the colonel."

"Who could?" The cook gathered up her basket and appeared to be about to leave.

Forsythe used the same tactic on her as he did on Sandy when she was reluctant to confide. He gave all of his attention to the smoke trailing from the pipe bowl. It worked. "Killed his wife, he did. Cruel man! Made the kiddies' lives hell. Drove Mister Charles away, and he died too. Spent all his life punishing Miss Honoria."

"I imagine he held her responsible for her mother's death."

"That and other things. Pray for him every night, I do."

Forsythe blinked. "For Colonel Farquson?"

"Get down on my knees and pray. Say to the Lord, Keep that sinner burning in hell! Fry him good!" Turning her back, she moved away like a small galleon breasting the sea. Black draperies wafted behind her. So did a few words. "Evil shall be punished, I always say."

Indeed it should, Forsythe thought, but the sad fact is that it seems to happen so infrequently. Punishment appears to be meted out, quite unfairly, to the good—to people like Honoria Farquson who gave up a winter coat so an old widow would be warm.

Leaving the kitchen garden, Forsythe set off toward the lime trees. When he reached them he found they'd been planted in a double line. The boy from the village had not been cutting here, and grass, high and lush and damp, was knee-high. Someone had come this way before him. In places the tall grass was tramped down into a tangled mat. When he came out in a sunny clearing he could see the summer house. It was whimsical and had a roof like a pagoda with heavy pillars supporting it. He mounted shallow steps and found Honoria spreading a checkered cloth and Sandy holding a wicker basket in one hand and a pitcher tinkling with ice in the other.

"Where have you been?" Miss Sanderson demanded.

"Lost my way and had to ask directions. Mrs. Potter and I had a little chat."

"Potty?" Taking the basket, Honoria set it down and started to unpack it. "She must have taken a fancy to you. Seldom Potty speaks to anyone but Potter and me."

"She wasn't exactly talkative. How are you feeling, Miss Farquson?"

She lifted her face and that face was composed, with no sign of swollen eyes or tears. But the cornflower eyes looked older, immeasurably saddened. "I'm coping, Mr. Forsythe. Life must go on and I have guests to look after. Unfortunately I'm losing the maids and if Abigail hadn't offered to help out I don't know what I would do. You've both been very kind."

"The chief inspector has agreed the girls may go?"

"He was far from eager to send them back to the village but Chief Inspector Kepesake realized Edie couldn't be kept on. That child has always been a timid, flighty girl and she's convinced she's in danger here. Sarah was willing to remain but I feel her place is with her sister. Now do eat, Mr. Forsythe, we must keep up our strength."

Nothing loath, Forsythe helped himself generously to cold roast beef, vegetable salad, and accepted a glass of lemonade from Miss Sanderson. Honoria extended a plate of rolls. "Do have one. They're freshly baked. What did you and Potty find to talk about?"

"This and that. The villagers down at the gates and your father."

A wan smile touched the woman's lips. "Did she tell you about her prayers? Ah, she did. Potty fancies herself as a devout Christian. Both she and Potter come from chapel families, yet she sees nothing wrong in asking for the poor colonel's soul to burn for eternity."

"Poor?" Miss Sanderson asked sharply.

"A bare recital of the colonel's life is not fair to the man.

101

You must remember he was a professional soldier, accustomed to command, and he retired too early. He was miffed at being passed over for promotion. The colonel had private means and he was financially secure but here he was on this estate with only his two children. I'm afraid he did treat us as soldiers and demanded absolute obedience. Yes, he had a sad life. The colonel was quite incapable of loving and as a result he never knew what it was to be loved."

Miss Sanderson looked far from convinced and Forsythe hastened to say, "Mrs. Potter had a low opinion of Marcia Mather too."

One capable hand waved. "That was because of me. Marcia was a mischievous little girl and she did tend to get the musketeers in trouble. I remember once . . ." Her mouth softened and the cornflower eyes glinted with memory. "Marcia stole a bottle of liquor from Doctor Mather's cabinet. Gin, I believe. Your mother, Abigail, was having a garden party at the vicarage and Marcia poured the gin into the punch. It was some women's group being entertained, one connected with the church, of course. The ladies pronounced the punch delicious and drained the bowl. I understand Mrs. Jenkins, she was the butcher's wife, had to be carried home. That took a little doing as Mrs. Jenkins was a stout lady."

"Marcia blamed this on you?" Miss Sanderson asked.

"On your sister and me. The vicar was a man who believed in not sparing the rod—"

"I remember," Miss Sanderson said feelingly and touched her lean bottom.

"Teresa had to sit on a pillow for a week."

Forsythe pulled out his pipe and tobacco pouch. "Were you spanked?"

"The colonel didn't believe in corporal punishment. He watched and carefully decided what Charles and I were most fond of. In this case it was my pony. I called him

Butterscotch and I adored him. The morning after the garden party debacle I went to the stable to take him his carrot and Butterscotch's stall was empty. The colonel had arranged to sell him. He told me bad girls could not have ponies."

Forsythe neglected his pipe. He found he was hoping the cook's stern God was listening to her prayers. "So, Marcia was a troublemaker."

"In a way. But she was such a high-spirited girl and so pretty, much prettier than Teresa or I. I remember her hair. Her mother trained it into ringlets and it was thick and such a lovely chestnut color. How Teresa and I envied those ringlets. Teresa had barely a wave in her hair and mine was as straight as string." She touched fine, silver-gilt hair and sighed. "Such dreamers the three of us were. Teresa called us the dream makers, but Marcia always insisted we must work to make our dreams come true."

Miss Sanderson propped her elbow on the table and turned toward the other woman. "What were the dreams?"

"You were never close to your sister as children, were you? And you spent so much time with your Aunt Rose. Well, Teresa dreamed of a life of wealth and ease."

"She certainly has that."

"Yes, and Marcia got her dream too. She wanted to be a beautiful, famous actress."

"And your dream?" Miss Sanderson asked softly.

"For a time I wanted to be an actress too. But I was greedy and wanted a husband as well, who would love me devotedly, and we'd have a large family. At times I had the number up to eight children and found names for all of them. Both Marcia and Teresa obtained their dreams. I never did."

"I wonder how happy it made them," Miss Sanderson mused. "Teresa seems terribly discontent."

"The only contentment the poor girl ever had was with

103

her first husband, but then she left him. Teresa went looking for Howard later, you know. After she lost her second husband . . . or was it the third? No matter. Teresa was heartbroken to find Howard had remarried, quite happily, and had children. As for Marcia, I think her life was as unhappy. When I met her again I found her cynical and rather callous." Honoria stared down at her plate. "Perhaps I was most fortunate. I never achieved my dream but for many years I still had it."

Forsythe asked gently, "You no longer do?"

Her mouth trembled. "My dreams died with Marcia, Mr. Forsythe. It's very hard to lose a childhood friend. One feels as though a part of one's past has also died." She glanced over his shoulder. "Mr. Cochrane, how nice of you to join us. Have you had lunch?"

The cameraman mounted the steps with his ponderous tread and lowered his bulk onto a bench facing the barrister. "Not yet. I came from another session with the police and it ruined my appetite."

Honoria set a plate in front of him and told him firmly, "You must eat something." She helped him liberally to meat and salad and placed a bun on the side of the plate. "Abigail and I have to get back to work, Mr. Cochrane, but this plate had better be emptied. Did Chief Inspector Kepesake give you a bad time?"

"Same questions as the other chief inspector asked last night but worded differently." Heavy shoulders moved in a shrug. "He got the same answers. Just came from the gates and all hell is breaking loose down there."

Honoria shook her shining head. "The public is so horribly morbid, isn't it?"

"Got a taste for blood all right." Cochrane's face split in a wide grin. "Looks like that mastiff of yours is better at crowd control than the constables are. He caught a reporter trying to climb over the wall and had at him."

"I do hope Heathcliff didn't injure him."

"Only his pride and one pant leg but my guess is it'll be a while before anyone else tries."

Honoria had finished repacking the basket and Miss Sanderson tipped the pitcher over Cochrane's glass. "Bit weak, Sam, the ice has melted down."

"It's wet and that's all that matters." Cochrane drank thirstily. Over the rim of the glass he watched the women making their way toward the double lines of limes. "For their age those two move pretty spryly."

Forsythe had also been watching them. Sandy walked along with her easy loping stride and Honoria took shorter, running steps, but they both covered ground rapidly. "They're not exactly ancient. Miss Farquson is on the sunny side of fifty."

"And Abigail?"

"Anyone's guess and knowing Sandy that's all it ever will be."

The cameraman seemed to have recovered his appetite. He was devouring his lunch. "Didn't mention it in front of Honoria but those villagers are having a time down there. Seem to be split into two factions. One group, led by a man who says he's a pig farmer and looks the part, is declaring in front of cameras that this estate is Sodom and Gomorrah and those scarlet sinners—that's our film group—are up to every imaginable orgy. The other bunch has appointed the local grocer as spokesman and he's refuting the pig farmer. According to the grocer Miss Farquson is an angel and nothing sinful would ever go on around her. The only point they appear to agree on is that the colonel was the devil incarnate."

"Amen to that," Forsythe said, thinking of a pony named Butterscotch. "Any idea how Dowling is making out?"

"As far as I know he's still barricaded in the late devil's room with Erika trotting trays back and forth to him."

Cochrane grinned again but this time there was no humor in it. "Knowing Mickey I'd imagine she's also acting as royal food taster. Mickey would put anyone's neck but his on the chopping block and Erika's going right along with it. Playing a new role—this one of mother protecting her young."

At the man's tone Forsythe's eyes fastened on him. "I thought you liked Erika."

"Like her? I guess you'd say I love her, in a fatherly way of course. And, as you probably know by now, that's one role I'm not qualified to play. I remember the first time I saw the little girl. In Hollywood, of course, I've done most of my work there. Erika was about nine and Mel and I were both working on her second film. Queer little kid. Those were the days when child actresses had a lot of blonde curls and did cute little songs and dances. Not Erika. Went straight into dramatic roles and could she portray genuine childhood. All the fears and doubts and frustrations . . . sad little kid."

"Why do you call her sad?"

Leaning back on the bench, Cochrane searched in a pocket. Sunlight fell across his face and displayed fine lines the barrister hadn't noticed previously. "Do you have cigarettes, Robert? Oh, I forgot. You stick to a pipe. Not to worry, I smoke too much anyway. Yes, sad Erika. You'd have to know her mother to understand. Mind, I liked Von Farquson, but Lord, what a driver that woman was! Lousy actress but she knew talent when she saw it. Von used to talk a lot about her brother and what a loss it was to the stage when Erik Larsen died. Anyway, she spotted the same talent in her young daughter and the kid never had a chance. Came straight out of diapers into drama school and that was it."

He'd finally found a crumpled package and a lone cigarette. Forsythe lit it for him and he leaned back. "Little girl grew up lopsided. Never had a normal childhood, no time for games or being young. Von took good care of her. Looked after Erika like a valuable racehorse—proper diet, proper grooming, that sort of thing. When Erika should have been playing with dolls and looking forward to boyfriends, she was learning lines and working like a pint-sized demon. I blame that childhood for her falling for Mickey Darling."

"I've followed her career with a great deal of interest and through the years her name has been linked romantically with a number of her leading men and also that professional tennis player."

"Publicity. Nothing more. Von was careful that her daughter didn't get involved with a man. Might have felt it would weaken her hold on the girl. Von died about three years ago. Had hypertension, a woman like that is a candidate for that sort of thing. I've always thought her death was . . . fitting."

"How did she die?"

"In the middle of a furious fight over contracts with a studio head. Von's eyes rolled up and she keeled over, heart attack. For the first time in her life Erika was on her own and she wasted no time. Fell head over heels for Dowling. Couldn't have made a worse choice."

Forsythe was frowning. "That certainly doesn't sound lopsided."

"What I omitted to say is Erika's playing the role of a woman with her first love. Like the role she played when her aunt came to London—dutiful loving niece."

"Aren't you being unnecessarily harsh?"

"Told you I love the girl. It's not her fault she can only counterfeit emotions. Erika's like a—" He broke off, his wide forehead furrowed with thought. "Like a mirror. Reflects what it sees but feels nothing itself. Still, she's a dangerous woman. Men always pounding themselves against her, trying to crack that exterior. Maybe it's a good thing she picked on Mickey. At least she can't hurt him." Cochrane glanced at his companion's frowning face and added, "Only my opinion, Robert, and I could be wrong. God knows I've been before."

His daughter Jenny, Forsythe thought, and that's what I'd better get him talking about. "I think you're being unnecessarily harsh with yourself too, Sam."

Bitter lines were etched at the corners of the big man's mouth. For a time he was silent and Forsythe was beginning to think he was to have no more luck with Cochrane than Chief Inspector Parker had had. Then Cochrane said slowly, "I can never be harsh enough with myself. Since Jenny's death I've tried blaming Marcia for not looking after her better, the housekeeper for being slack, even the police for not finding the man who did it. In the end, I'm the one to blame."

"The police. Did they never get any leads?"

"None. Whoever did it covered his tracks."

"What about those friends of your daughter, the ones who helped alibi her?"

"They couldn't give the police any help. I had a go at them myself thinking they'd talk to me. Found out they had nothing to tell. All Jenny told the other girls was that the man she'd fallen for was 'an older guy' and 'thrilling.' To a girl of sixteen any man over twenty is an older man. Thrilling? Who knows how a little girl would mean that?" Cochrane shifted on the wooden bench and pushed his plate away. "My wife was killed the day before Jenny's fourth birthday. Hit-and-run driver. Never found him either. There I was, left with a little kid. Marcia had been Meg's best friend and she thought the world of little Jenny so between us we tried to raise the kid. Pretty little thing, fair, with eyes like her mother. Used to tease Jenny about looking like her mother. Told her it was a good thing she didn't take after me. Never gave a lick of trouble. Quiet and well-behaved."

The cameraman stopped and buried his face in his hands. His voice was muffled as he said, "Couldn't believe it when I got that wire. I thought some horrible mistake had been made. Always thought of Jenny as a child. Wasn't until I saw her on the slab in the morgue that I realized she had developed a woman's body."

Forsythe regarded the man with compassion and, hating himself for it, asked a question. "You didn't believe the rumors that Michael Dowling was implicated?"

"Didn't believe or disbelieve. Didn't know. Rumors came mainly from Marcia and she wasn't above lying about him. Couldn't see how it *could* be him. Sure, Jenny tagged around after him but a lot of girls do. Dowling treated Jenny the same as the others, teased her and kidded with her. For God's sake, Robert, he'd known her since she was ten!"

Cochrane lumbered to his feet and Forsythe said, "Have you stopped looking for the man?"

"Never will. Only thing keeping me alive."

The barrister watched him move slowly toward the lime trees. Before Cochrane reached them another man, this one quick-moving, darted out of the shadow into the sunny glade. Sun glinted dazzlingly from Melvin Borthwick's naked skull. He paused to speak to his friend, and then made for the summer house. Before he reached Forsythe he was talking. "Damn wretches! Wrung me dry. Feel like I've been put through a meat grinder. Told them the same things over and over."

Forsythe grinned. "I take it you've been interviewed by the men from London."

"You take it right and that was no interview. More of an endurance test. Stupid questions. Was I on the first floor after we came back from Koster's greenhouse? Told the ruddy fools of course I was. Only bathroom in the house is up there. Did I see anyone else? Anyone acting suspiciously?" Flopping down in Cochrane's place, the little man pulled out a silver flask. He picked up Cochrane's glass, threw a few drops of liquid over his shoulder, and poured from the flask. He shoved it over to Forsythe. "My own stock. Cross my heart I haven't poisoned it." As though to demonstrate his point he tipped up the flask and took a long swallow. Then he grudgingly added, "Shouldn't blame the police. Be glad to see them get to the bottom of this. Any idea when they'll let us go, Robert?"

"After the inquest, but I've no idea when that will be."

"Damnation! We've got to get back to London. Murder or no murder this film has got to be kept on schedule."

"You are going on with it?"

"Why not?"

"Well, Marcia . . ."

"Marcia only had a small part. Can get another actress or write the part out." Borthwick stretched and said expansively, "Believe it or not but Marcia dead is going to give it a boost she never could in life. May sound callous but that's show biz. Mickey has the most incredible *luck*. This murder is going to bring the public out in droves. The film will be a blockbuster." Borthwick gazed at his companion and said, "Come on now, old boy, don't look so disapproving."

"Not disapproving, simply stunned. I knew the woman for a couple of days and I *feel* something. You knew her for years and—"

"—feel like hell about her death. We'll go to her funeral and send flowers and do some mourning for her—when we have time. Now we've got a picture to film. Marcia would have acted the same way. We're professionals." The director looked around discontentedly. "Had a dandy scene slated for this spot and now we can't use the place. Have to find somewhere else and keep the location quiet. Sightseers will run all over us if we don't."

110

"Does Miss Farquson know about the change in location?"

"Told her before I came out and you know what she offered? To give me my advance back. Said it might take a while to come up with the money because she'd used it for the maids' salaries and extra food. What a lady!"

"Are you going to take her money?"

"I said we're professionals, not Shylocks. Of course I'm not taking the poor lady's money. I told Honoria that advance was in the nature of an option and she'd done her part. I wish for her sake we were filming here. Honoria could certainly use the money. That maid, the little one who threw screaming meemies, told me they'd heard in the village that Honoria and the Potters spent last winter living in the kitchen and a couple of other rooms. Couldn't afford the fuel to keep the rest of the place heated. She said the villagers figured the colonel had made bad investments on purpose just to impoverish his daughter."

"I heard something about that myself." Forsythe added casually, "Sam Cochrane was telling me about Erika."

Although his voice was casual he couldn't have schooled his expression as successfully. Borthwick's bright little eyes, under the beetling brows, swung shrewdly toward the barrister. "Told you something you didn't care for, eh?"

"Sam said she's lopsided. Do you agree?"

"With the term, no. With what old Sam's trying to say, yes. I've always thought of Erika as a series of roles, one on top of the other. You peel them off and underneath is . . . emptiness, a vacuum. Tell you what, you want an authority on Erika Von Farr, check it out with Giles."

"He's in love with her," Forsythe said dully.

"And knows he's a damn fool but can't help himself." Borthwick hopped up. "Better get in and stir things up. Try to pin that Kepesake down on when he'll let us go. He had Giles on the griddle when I left the house. Next one in line

111

is Mickey." A broad smile twitched at the bushy mustache. "Want to make any bets on whether the chief inspector goes up to Mickey or Mickey comes down to him?"

"Not interested."

Forsythe didn't bother lifting his head as the director left. He stared morosely down into his untouched drink. What did men who considered a friend's death good publicity know about an intense, sensitive girl like Erika Von Farr? Couldn't see the forest for the trees, too close to her to realize her emotions were genuine. Erika *did* care for her aunt, *did* love Michael Dowling. Good Lord, Forsythe thought, I'm half in love with her.

He sat brooding, unaware of time passing. When he lifted his head the shadows were lengthening. He checked his watch. Tea time. To his surprise he found he was hungry again. Tossing Borthwick's liquor on the grass, he gathered together the plates and cutlery used by Cochrane and piled them up. Carrying them, he headed down the double row of limes.

CHAPTER NINE

As Forsythe entered the front door he spotted the detectives from London coming down the staircase. Kepesake was in the lead and not only was his hair mussed but he looked choleric. Behind him Sergeant Brummell wore a wide grin. Over his superior's shoulder he winked at the barrister. The chief inspector glared at Forsythe and pointed at the plates in his hands. "Acting as a domestic, Forsythe?"

"Doing my bit to help out," Forsythe told him amiably.

Keeping his voice low, Kepesake broke into a stream of curses, all of them directed at the film industry in general and actors in particular. "Wouldn't set a foot out of that room," he sputtered. "Only way I could have got him down here was have a couple of constables carry him. Of all the jackasses!"

"You've interviewed Michael Dowling?"

"Now I'm certain he *was* the intended victim and I can see why. Much more of him and I'd start sympathizing with the murderer."

Chief Inspector Parker had joined them and was trying,

unsuccessfully, to hide a grin. "Tsk, tsk, unprofessional conduct."

Kepesake turned the glare on his colleague. "Thought you'd left for Elleston."

"On my way, but I waited to hear if you'd picked up anything new from Dowling."

"Same thing he gave you last night. Appears to put undue attention on the most ridiculous trifles. Kept harping away because he broke that glass—" Breaking off, Kepesake looked suddenly thoughtful. "A trifle. Your field, Forsythe. Think there could be anything in it?"

The barrister didn't bother hiding his grin. "I hardly think it pertinent."

"Wanted me to leave bodyguards for him," Kepesake raged on. "Two! One man to sit beside his bed, the other posted with his back against the door."

Sergeant Brummell spoke to Forsythe. "Told the chief it wasn't a bad idea. Someone might have another go at Dowling."

"And how are they going to reach him, Beau?" Kepesake demanded. "He's locked behind two inches of solid oak with Miss Farr on guard. Dowling's safe enough.

"Of course I'm taking reasonable precautions. There'll be constables on the gates and a couple of others on the grounds. Parker's man, Summer, will be in the house until six and he'll be relieved by another man. Did you pick a good one, Chief Inspector Parker?"

"My best. Constable Jenkins."

Forsythe raised his brows. "This constable wouldn't by any chance be related to the people who ran the butcher shop at one time?"

"Still do. At least Constable Jenkin's brother has it now. They're grandsons of the original owners." Parker gave the barrister an admiring look. "You really do pick up on trifles, don't you?"

"Heard the names earlier today. Seems Grandmother Jenkins was carried home in her cups from a garden party at the vicarage."

Parker laughed. "Hardly sounds like the Jenkins family. They're chapel and teetotalers."

"Mrs. Jenkins had no idea she was swilling gin with the punch."

Parker was still smiling but Kepesake pushed past them, one hand smoothing down his ruffled locks. "We'll be in Bury-Sutton at the inn there. Hear it's not bad. What's the name, Beau?"

"The Unicorn, chief."

"Right. Don't hesitate to ring us up, Forsythe, if you think of anything."

"Don't bank on it. I'm as much at sea as you are."

The chief inspector took Beau's arm. "Come on. Speaking of sea we're going to be breasting a rough tide at the gates with the media."

"Issuing a statement, chief?"

"Guess we'll have to." Kepesake struck a pose. "We have several promising leads and are following them up. Developments expected momentarily."

"Hogwash," Parker muttered in Forsythe's ear and followed the other two officers.

The barrister realized he was still balancing the plates. He looked around, shrugged, and deposited them on the telephone table. Then, wanting his tea, he headed hopefully toward the closed doors of the drawing room. Behind those doors was a peaceful tableau. Honoria Farquson presided over the tea table; Giles leaned nonchalantly against the mantel; and Miss Sanderson was stretching her long legs out to the circle of warmth cast by a crackling wood fire.

Forsythe sniffed the pleasant odor permeating the room. "Smells like apple wood."

"How discerning," his hostess said. "I thought it would

115

make a nice touch. It was a windfall from last autumn. I had our boy from the village split the tree up. At one time there was quite a nice orchard near the gatehouse. Perhaps you noticed the trees." She sighed. "They're all very old now and haven't been tended properly. I suppose they should come down but I rather dread to have it done. Do sit and have your tea, Mr. Forsythe. Have the police left yet?"

Taking a chair beside his secretary, Forsythe stretched out his bad leg toward the warmth of the apple wood fire. "They were leaving when I came in. Chief Inspector Kepesake and his sergeant are staying at the Unicorn in Bury-Sutton."

"They'll be comfortable there. Lydia Preston is a good cook and the rooms, though small, are clean. I do hope they're leaving the policemen at the gates. Heaven knows what those curiosity seekers will get up to if no one is there."

"The chief inspector told me the gates will be guarded, the grounds patrolled, and one man will be left in the house. The name of the constable on night duty is Jenkins. Perhaps you know him."

"Indeed I do. He was in my Sunday school class at one time. A nice little boy but shy. I've often thought it was that unfortunate name his mother Arabella wished on him that made him bashful. Absolem! The other boys teased him about it unmercifully."

Forsythe accepted his cup and examined the bountiful tea spread out before him. It was as lavish as the one provided the day before at the Koster cottage. "Are Borthwick and Cochrane joining us?"

Giles smiled. "Sam is upstairs now and I guess Mel has probably joined him. Mel's been ringing up London with a constable hanging over him listening to every word. Putting the pressure on at the studio to have the legal department get us out of here. We are supposed to be back at the studio

116

tomorrow morning. Did the police give you any idea, Robert, when we're being released from bondage?"

"I've no more idea than the rest of you."

"Come now, I'm sure you do."

"Exactly what do you mean by that?"

"You and Kepesake are buddies. He was the officer in charge on that moor murder you solved last year. Come on, open up."

It was Miss Sanderson who said tartly, "Even if Robby has been taken into the chief inspector's confidence do you think he'd be free to tell us anything?"

"Sorry. Guess I'm a bid edgy." The young man's freckled face turned toward their hostess. "Mickey and Erika coming down for dinner?"

"I'm afraid not, Mr. Eady. I did try to persuade them this afternoon to join us. Mickey says he'll be more comfortable in the colonel's quarters. Why I can't understand. It's a gloomy place. Mickey is being such a silly boy."

"This time I don't blame our golden boy. Someone did try to knock him off, you know."

"Nonsense! I'm certain the police will find it was simply a tragic accident."

Giles had been swallowing his tea and now he choked. "*Accident*. My dear lady, you think the cyanide got into Mickey's bottle by accident?"

She considered this and then said slowly, "That is a little difficult to accept, isn't it? Perhaps an absolute stranger crept into the house and put poison into the whiskey. After all, there are many demented people with grudges against public personages."

The writer was regarding her with something approaching admiration. "That theory would get us all off the hook and I'm rather taken with it. But how was this stranger, demented or otherwise, going to get past the noble Heathcliff? That brute would have had him in several pieces."

117

"Heathcliff could have been drugged by one of those tranquilizing guns one sees on television."

"I'm beginning to think you have the makings of a writer. All right, Heathcliff is drugged. The demented stranger sneaks into the house, goes immediately to the right bedroom, and does the foul deed. Does that sound reasonable?"

Honoria was admitting there could be flaws in her reasoning, but at that moment she examined the Georgian teapot and jumped to her feet. "Dear me, quite dry. Excuse me a moment and I'll get hot water."

Forsythe glanced up. "I haven't seen Potter around today."

"I ordered him to bed, Mr. Forsythe. His back is giving him trouble again. He was reluctant to go, he's so conscientious, but Potty and I insisted."

Giles followed her with his eyes and when the door closed he said, "Know who she reminds me of?"

"A maiden aunt?" Miss Sanderson guessed.

"That woman in the old film, the one made during the war. Can't remember the actress's name . . ."

"Greer Garson," Forsythe said.

"That's it. Honoria Farquson is much like Mrs. Miniver, keeping an upper lip so stiff you'd think it starched. Carrying on magnificently while her world tumbles around her. Know what she told us about Mickey before you came in, Robert?"

Miss Sanderson chuckled. "Honoria said tomorrow that silly boy is joining us for dinner. She won't stand his foolishness any longer. Giles pointed out that two police forces couldn't budge him, but Honoria told us gently they weren't going about it the right way."

"This I'll have to see," Giles said. "The only way I can think of moving Mickey is by torching the house. Ah, here is fresh tea."

118

Honoria bustled in and set the pot down. "Your cup, Mr. Forsythe. Do have some of this quince preserve with your scone. I made it last fall and it did turn out well. I'm hoping we have a good crop of raspberries this year. I have a recipe for raspberry cordial, my grandmother's, that's quite tasty . . ."

The conversation turned to recipes and then, quite naturally, to gardening. Giles admitted he wouldn't know a turnip plant from a carrot but Forsythe was fairly knowledgeable. His grandmother, who Honoria reminded him of slightly, had insisted he help her with her beds. As a small boy his idol had been their brawny gardener and he'd tagged along behind the man. It was a peaceful time, and Forsythe found that with the crackling of the fire, Honoria's gentle voice, the play of light and shadow across the walls, tension drained from him. Finally, their hostess sent them upstairs to rest before dinner. Miss Sanderson didn't argue. "I'll be down to lay the table," she promised and leaned on the barrister's arm.

"Tired, Sandy?"

"Exhausted. Housework doesn't agree with me."

"With Aggie fussing over you I don't suppose you know much about that sort of thing."

"Dear old Aggie. I wish I had her fussing over me now. She has a sharp tongue but no one can complain about her cooking." They paused by Forsythe's door and Miss Sanderson asked, "Mind if I come in for a few minutes?"

In answer he swung the door wide. The room was dim and he reached for a lamp. Miss Sanderson shook her head. "No. It's peaceful this way." She curled up in an easy chair, her legs tucked up under her. "Tea time was peaceful too. I kept thinking all the rest of this had been a bad dream and we'd finally woken up. It doesn't seem possible a woman was murdered last evening."

Forsythe stretched out on the bed and stared up at the

ceiling. "In the words of Adam Kepesake, who certainly is not our buddy, have you any ideas?"

"If Marcia Mather wasn't dead, I'd pin it on her. She's my idea of the typical poisoner."

"Beau Brummell was playing with the thought that she might have killed herself to have Dowling brought up on a murder charge."

"Uh uh. She thought as much of her skin as Mickey Darling does. But I've narrowed the list of suspects down."

"Discarded Cochrane and Borthwick?"

"Robby, you can be infuriating! Always one jump ahead of me. I can't work either of those men in as suspects. Mel is so . . . shallow. There's hate connected with this crime and I don't think Mel could sustain hate or any other emotion for long."

"He could have had another motive."

"Erika Von Farr? Doesn't work. If he couldn't avenge his wife he's not going to kill for Erika. Sam is more difficult. Let's say he's lying about not being sure Mickey was involved in his daughter's death. That would give him a gold-plated motive but I simply can't imagine him using poison. Sam would use his hands or perhaps a gun. Poison is so . . . so feminine."

"I suppose that eliminates Giles Eady too."

"Giles is still in the running. He has a feminine streak. I don't mean he's effeminate, and on the surface he's bright and glib and amusing but there's a touch of female spite in some of the things he says. And I've seen him looking at Erika. Yes, I think for her Giles could kill. My next suspect is Honoria—"

"Now you have surprised me, Sandy. I should have thought Honoria would be the first person you'd cross off the suspect list."

"I have taken the Potters off it. Honoria would have had to urge them on and she's far too fine and honorable to do that. Yet, oddly enough, I can see her doing it. Where I fall down is motive."

"Erika is her niece and Dowling . . . well, he's Dowling."

In her shadowed corner Miss Sanderson stirred. It was too dark to see her face but Forsythe had a feeling she was frowning. Then he heard a tiny click and smiled. Sandy must be deep in thought. She was clicking her thumbnail against her front teeth. After a moment she said, "Honoria saw her niece for the first time in thirty years barely a month ago. She may have loved baby Erika but I've the impression she feels little for the adult Erika. As I said, we're dealing with hate. To hate that much there has to be strong emotion. I simply don't feel Honoria loves her niece enough to kill for her. And she did give her consent to the marriage and promised the estate as a wedding present. Honoria would keep a promise."

"That leaves Erika Von Farr."

His secretary made no answer and he propped himself up on an elbow and switched on the bedside lamp. The bulb cast a circle of light on his face but Miss Sanderson's was still obscure. He switched it off. "That verse from Coleridge, Sandy, was that aimed at Erika?"

"Anything I say will sound foolish. And I'm not foolish. I know I have a tendency to mother you, after all I did act as kind of a mother after your own died, but—"

"And did a good job, Sandy."

"Well, I'm not one of those maternal women who get all jealous and upset when their son looks at a woman. It's just . . . Robby, I don't want you hurt again."

Forsythe winced and closed his eyes. In his mind a picture formed, a girl's face, fine-featured, rather angelic. Virginia, he thought, who had proved the opposite of an angel. "That's all in the past," he said brusquely.

"Not that far in the past. Robby, I don't want you torn apart again."

"Be sensible, old girl. Erika Von Farr is simply an actress I happen to admire."

"More than admire. I blame this whole ungodly business on myself. I thought I was so clever bringing you together. Then I saw the look on your face."

"You make her sound like La Belle Dame sans Merci."

"No, not that."

"'Life-in-Death was she, Who thicks a man's blood with cold,'" he quoted.

"That's right, throw up a few lines I quoted at random. I didn't mean that either. It's simply that a woman can see Erika clearer than a man. She has an unfortunate effect on men. Turns them into gibbering idiots—"

"I am *not* a gibbering idiot."

"You feel something for her. Don't deny it. And she's bad news, Robby. Maybe because she seems unattainable. I feel she'd suck everything from a man, give nothing in return . . ."

"Now you're casting her as Countess Dracula."

"Will you shut up! Robby, Erika could well have put that poison in that bottle!"

"Give me one reason why."

"Very well." A muted click came from the shadows around his companion's chair. "Both Sam and Mel say Erika never looked at a man before Mickey Dowling hove into view. Devoted her entire life to her career. Nothing left over for romance. Out of the blue, she falls for a cad like Mickey. Why the sudden change?"

"Did they also tell you that her mother kept the girl away from males? Erika met Dowling after Von Farquson's death."

Sandy gave an unladylike snort. "Show me the red-blooded girl who a mother, domineering or otherwise, can keep away from men. And when Von died Erika was what—over twenty-seven? In a pig's eye! No, Erika has no interest in men. I don't think she loves Mickey; I think she's acting a part."

The barrister winced again and was glad his secretary couldn't see it. "Then why are they engaged, my wise old friend?"

"I think Mickey's holding something over her head, forcing her to marry him. He wouldn't be above a spot of blackmail, you know."

"What could there be in Erika's past to warrant blackmail? From the time she was a toddler she's been in the public domain. Her life is an open book."

"It could concern her mother."

"Same thing goes there too. And remember, Sandy, this is a permissive society we live in. There has to be something serious to warrant blackmail today. What could it be?"

"Murder? Perhaps Erika . . . no, that's too farfetched. Maybe something else. How about a hit-and-run and Mickey has proof Erika or her mother did it?" There was movement from Miss Sanderson's corner and a light went on bright enough to make the barrister blink. She was checking her watch. "Enough of crime, domestic duty calls. I have to whip around and dress and then I'll lay the table. Only be six of us tonight. Should make the washing up simpler."

She moved to the door and swung it open. As usual she had the last word. "Mark my word, Robby, when we get to the bottom of this we'll find Erika Von Farr right there."

CHAPTER TEN

THE NEXT MORNING FORSYTHE ROSE LATE. AS HE grunted his way to the window and pulled back the curtains his traveling clock said ten after ten. The day looked as gray and cheerless as he felt and when he lifted the sash a chill wind with the promise of rain made him thump down the pane. He knew he was too late for breakfast but he sought the breakfast room hoping for coffee. There he found not only coffee on the hotplate but Potter puttering around.

"Back better?" he asked.

"Quite recovered, sir. Mrs. Potter used liniment and Miss Honoria brought down her heating pad. Would you care for breakfast, sir?"

"Toast will be fine. I don't want to put Mrs. Potter to too much trouble."

"No trouble, sir." Potter paused beside the door and one eyelid flickered in something remarkably like a wink. "Mrs. Potter has taken a fancy to you, sir. London papers on the table if you'd care to look at them."

Forsythe pulled the papers over, wondering whether Potter *had* winked at him. He decided it must be a nervous tic. He glanced down at a front page, saw the lurid headlines, a row of photographs of Erika, Marcia, and Michael Dowling, and pushed them away. In a remarkably short time Potter trotted in bearing a platter. Looking down at the platter, Forsythe thought perhaps the cook *had* taken a fancy to him.

"Ah," the butler said, "Mrs. Potter thought you might care for blueberry waffles, sir."

"My favorite," Forsythe said and started to demolish not only waffles but scrambled eggs, tiny sausages, and rashers of bacon. He'd only made a start when Giles Eady lounged in.

"You look like I feel," the writer told him. "Bad night?"

"Rotten. Twisted and turned until after three and when I did get to sleep I had the worst nightmares in years."

"Hell of a day. Looks like rain." He glanced down at Forsythe's breakfast and his face brightened. "Hey, Potter, think your good wife could rustle up the same?"

"I doubt it, sir. Mrs. Potter's put away the waffle iron. I'll see what she can offer."

Giles stretched a hand out to the pile of newspapers. "Jesus! Well, I suppose you can't expect anything else. Listen to this. 'Police are searching for the fiend who slew the beautiful actress Marcia Mather.' Make it sound like a sex crime. Ah, honorable mention for you and Abigail. 'Robert Forsythe, barrister and private detective, is working with the police on this horrible crime. His secretary Miss Abigail Sanderson, is also assisting. A breakthrough is expected at any moment.' No picture of Giles Eady, famous writer. Let's see, more photographs on page four. Here I am, and so is Mel, and Sam Cochrane, looking remarkably like a water buffalo. They've got a good shot of this house and a blurry one of Honoria where she looks about fifteen." He threw the papers on the floor. "Wish that breakthrough would happen and we could get out of here. Know what our boys in blue are up to now?"

"Didn't see any of them when I came down."

"Searching the bedrooms. Practically yanked me out of mine and I'd swear the constable went through the pockets of my jeans before he handed them over. Of all the—" Breaking off, he smiled. "Breakfast." His smile disappeared. "An egg and a slice of toast!"

"It is late, sir," Potter told him frigidly and made his departure.

Giles cast a disconsolate glance at Forsythe. He was spearing a bit of waffle. "Teacher's pet. Been buttering up the cook, eh?"

"Not guilty."

"That old world charm of yours."

Forsythe cut into a sausage. "Should cultivate some yourself. You'd eat better. Did the police say what they're looking for?"

"Thought you could tell me that but I guess you won't squeal on your buddies. Can't be large. They shook out the books on my bedtable."

Small enough, Forsythe thought, to be hidden under Marcia Mather's handkerchiefs. "Any sign of Mickey this morning?"

"I suppose he's still locked in. Saw Erika in the hall. She looks like a ghost and I tried to get her to come out for a breath of air but she brushed me off."

Forsythe rose to refill his coffee cup. Giles's prediction was coming true; drops of rain pattered against the window. He said casually, "When we were reading characters from faces the other evening you said Erika was the simplest of all."

"She's an actress."

"What does that signify?"

"Exactly what I said. First, last, and in the middle, the girl is an actress." The writer shoved his plate away and looked moodily at the wet panes. "Take my advice, Robert,

126

and don't get any yearnings for the lass. I keep following her about knowing I'm mad to do it and can't help myself. Falling in love with Erika is like having the seven-year itch and both hands tied."

"You knew her mother?"

"Von? Certainly. She trailed after Erika like a bloodhound. Why?"

"Were either of them in London twelve years ago?"

The other man's face was perplexed. "How would I know?"

"Someone—I think it was Dowling—said this is the first time Erika's been in England. What about her mother?"

"As far as I know Erika's never been in England before. Von was all over the place; she acted as her daughter's agent, you know. She could have been here. What has twelve years ago got to do with this murder?"

"Possibly nothing. But you're a writer. Figure it out."

Giles thought, drumming his freckled fingers on the table. "Murder . . . roots in the past. But Erika and Von? Robert, Von's dead."

"Erika isn't."

"What could have happened that long ago? Something still important to one of us. Give me a hint."

Silently, Forsythe debated. He needed this man's help. Coming to a decision he said, "Sam Cochrane."

"Sam." The other man chewed his lower lip. "Got it! Meg Cochrane killed twelve years ago by a hit-and-run driver. She was thrown against a curb and her neck snapped. The bastard didn't even stop. But Von or Erika had nothing to do with that."

"Are you certain?"

"By now you have me so confused I'm not certain of my own name. Okay, you win. I'll ask around. Find out where they were on the exact date. Better not ask Sam. I'll have a go at Mel and see whether he remembers." Getting up, he

127

clapped Forsythe's shoulder. "Just joined your club. Now I'm a detective."

Or a murderer, Forsythe thought dourly. The door opened again and this time Constable Summer's ruddy face poked around the panel. "Chief Inspector Kepesake would like to speak to you when you have a moment, sir."

Both chief inspectors were in the library. The room looked smaller. The bookcases were bare and their contents were piled helter-skelter over the carpet. From the wall over the fireplace Colonel Farquson seemed to glower at this desecration. Behind the desk Kepesake was also glowering. He greeted the barrister with an impatient, "Sit down and take a look at the autopsy report."

Forsythe picked his way through the tumble of books, took a seat, and accepted the report. "Any luck with the search?"

"Not so far. Would help if the lads knew what they were looking for."

Bending his head, Forsythe scanned the pathologist's findings. Cause of death . . . probable time of death . . . woman of forty-nine in good condition . . . organs healthy . . . slight anemic condition . . . congestion in the nasal passages. He passed it back to Kepesake. "No help there."

"No help here either." Kepesake thumped a fist on the piles of paper scattered untidily in front of him. "Backgrounds on everyone in the house. Not much here we haven't already got."

Chief Inspector Parker brushed at his thin mustache. "One interesting item about Michael Dowling. The teacher who financed his trip to Los Angeles doesn't seem to have done it willingly. Miss Pike's dead but one of Dowling's school friends says he remembers the man—or boy as he was then—bragging about squeezing money from the woman. This chap said Dowling and Miss Pike were having a hot affair and Dowling managed to get a snapshot of her in the altogether. Threatened to show it to the school board if she didn't hand over her savings."

"Nasty piece of goods," Kepesake said. "But it doesn't have any bearing on Miss Mather's death."

"It does prove he's capable of blackmail," Forsythe mentioned.

"If he's capable of drug dealing he's capable of anything," Kepesake said dourly. "Slippery devil. Narcotics is positive he's bringing the stuff in but can't pin him down. Smarter than he acts."

"He *is* an actor," Parker pointed out.

"Don't belabor the obvious." Kepesake picked up a sheet and frowned at it. "This is the report on Melvin Borthwick. I can see why his wife's affair with Dowling didn't bother him very much. That director is a great man for the ladies. Had one affair after another, before his marriage, during it, and after his wife's suicide. His latest girl friend is a young fashion model who appears to think she'll be the next Mrs. Borthwick. If I were her I wouldn't hold my breath."

Forsythe leaned forward. "Nothing else on Borthwick?"

Parker grinned. "This group of people are really tangled up. At one time Veronica Larsen Farquson was Borthwick's mistress. Years ago, of course."

"Erika's mother," Forsythe muttered. "What about Samuel Cochrane?"

"Not a single black mark. Only women in his life were his wife and daughter. Margaret Cochrane was his childhood sweetheart; they married young, and Cochrane never seems to have even looked at another woman."

Kepesake was still frowning. "Same goes for Honoria Farquson. Life's an open book. The only time she's been away from this estate is for about five weeks when she was—"

"Eighteen," Forsythe said.

"And for about seven months when she was abroad with her sister-in-law. In Colonel Farquson's lifetime the farthest afield she went was to Elleston to shop. Five weeks ago she went to London to meet her niece but she was only there for three days. She had no prior connection with any of these people except Marcia Mather in her childhood and, of course, Erika and Abigail Sanderson." Kepesake transferred his frown to the other chief inspector. "I'm willing to admit Miss Farquson is out of it and—" He broke off and asked brusquely, "What is it now, Summer?"

Summer, wearing a smile, was in the doorway. "MacDonald and Barry have run into trouble in the kitchen, sir. The cook is objecting to them searching her cupboards. Mrs. Potter has both of them backed into a corner."

"Dear Lord." Kepesake gazed at the ceiling as though for help and then waved his jade holder at the grinning constable. "Surely two good-sized men can handle a frail old lady."

"The frail old lady is brandishing a meat cleaver, sir."

Kepesake seemed speechless but Parker, grinning as widely as the constable, told him, "Better have Miss Farquson speak to the old girl."

Kepesake inserted a fresh cigarette in his holder. "This ruddy case! A cook attacking my men with cleavers, an actor locked in a bedroom, that Eady quoting Shakespeare, the police commissioner on my back . . ."

"You've many problems," Forsythe observed without the slightest trace of sympathy.

Kepesake continued with his litany of woes. "Lawyers from the legal department of the studio swarming all over, Dowling's fan clubs sending wires threatening mayhem if one hair of their idol's head is hurt, the media demanding a quick solution. We damn well are having our problems, Forsythe, and you're not raising a finger to be of help."

Sighing heavily, he searched through the disorder on the desk. "Erika Von Farr. Until she met Michael Dowling not a hint about men in her life. Those romances in the gossip columns appear to be straight fabrications cooked up by publicity departments."

"Any information about the finances of these people?" Forsythe asked.

"Yes, a complete rundown. Now who the hell is it this time? Oh, Beau. Thank God you've rustled up some food. Set it down, man. I'm starved."

Sergeant Brummell jerked a nod at Forsythe and put down the tray. "Couldn't manage much, chief. Sandwiches and beer. Kitchen's been in an uproar."

Parker opened a bottle of beer and poured it foaming into a glass. "Did Summer bring Miss Farquson in on it?"

"Few minutes ago. Miss Farquson herded the old girl into her bedroom. Hope she's locked in. All quiet on the kitchen front now, but that cook's a terror. Mrs. Potter doesn't reach MacDonald's shoulder and she had him quaking. Care for a sandwich, Mr. Forsythe?"

The barrister declined and turned back to Kepesake. "What about the finances?"

Kepesake spoke thickly around a mouthful of sandwich. "Tell him, Beau."

"Most of them in good shape. Mr. Borthwick lives above his means and has debts but nothing horrific. Miss Farr has a bundle, most of it invested in property in the Los Angeles area. Michael Dowling is loaded. Among other things he has a controlling interest in a soft drink concern and in one of those fast food chains. Seems to have an obsession with money. Can't get enough. Rumor is he's trying to get Miss Farr to come in with him on some hotel deal."

Wiping off his mustache, Parker asked, "Any luck with the search, sergeant?"

"Not so far and I doubt the lads will turn anything up.

131

Figure whatever it was is long gone. There's a fireplace in nearly every room in this house. Could have been burned or flushed down the w.c." Brummell scrubbed at his shaggy hair. "Good chance it has nothing to do with Miss Mather's death."

Kepesake stared at his sergeant. "What are you getting at?"

"Figure one of these people here knew Miss Mather had something with her he didn't want found when they went through her belongings. Could have been . . . maybe love letters."

Kepesake gave an undignified snort. "With these weirdies I'm willing to wager any love letters would be read by them in Hyde Park to as large an audience as possible."

"Maybe so, chief. Hey, could have been a snapshot."

"In that case they'd be willing to publish it in a paper. I think you're reaching, Beau. The search of the dead woman's room is definitely tied up with the crime." Daintily wiping his finger tips, Kepesake reached for his cigarette holder. "Any ideas yet, Forsythe?"

"Let's get back to Cochrane. Are you certain he wasn't involved with another woman? I'm thinking of Von Farquson."

"If he was it was kept very quiet." Kepesake leaned forward and looked hopefully at the barrister. "What are you thinking?"

"It was Miss Sanderson's idea. She mentioned a hit-and-run accident and I thought immediately of Meg Cochrane. Could you find out when the accident happened and where Von Farquson and Erika Von Farr were on that date?"

Eagerly the chief inspector scrabbled through the papers on the desk. The room was blue with cigarette smoke and Brummell coughed and opened a window a crack. A frosty gust of wind blew in and rustled the papers. Kepesake said irritably, "Will you shut that damned window? All I need now is pneumonia. Hmm, the death of Cochrane's wife occurred in . . . let's see—"

"Twelve years ago," Forsythe told him.

"Right. May the twelfth. You're figuring Veronica Farquson could have eliminated a rival. Well, I can find out where she was at the time. But her daughter . . . Miss Farr was definitely in Hollywood working on a film. I don't get the tie with her."

"Miss Sanderson found it odd that an actress so devoted to her career would suddenly lose her head over a man like Dowling and put that career in jeopardy."

Kepesake bit his lip and Brummell said, "I've seen level-headed women lose their heads over worthless men before this, Mr. Forsythe."

Kepesake looked hopeful. "You think Dowling might be blackmailing Miss Farr about her mother? He blackmailed before, when he was only a boy. It's possible. We'll check it out. Anything further?"

"A couple of points puzzle me. But first I'd like to ask *you* a question. Is the date for the inquest set yet?"

Brummell chuckled and Parker asked, "Using a spot of blackmail yourself, counselor?"

"If he is, he's too late. Someone got there before you, Forsythe," Kepesake told him. "The studio head happens to be a member of the same club as the police commissioner. Orders have come down to let these film people get back to work. So . . . the inquest is slated for tomorrow afternoon at three. It will be held in Elleston and transportation will be laid on for all of you. Afterward you can go back to your vacation."

"Any objection if I go to Scotland?"

"Not as long as you leave the address and a number where you can be reached. Now give."

Templing his fingers, Forsythe gazed at them. "Miss Sanderson said she didn't believe Honoria Farquson thought

133

highly of Michael Dowling. The first day I arrived I sensed nothing but dislike for the man from her. Yet, she swings right around, starts calling him Mickey, gives her consent to her niece's marriage, and is going to deed over this estate to Dowling. Something fishy there."

"Blackmail," Parker said hotly. "Miss Farquson has nothing to hide."

"But maybe Miss Farr has," Brummell said. "And it could be tied in with her mother like Mr. Forsythe said." He turned to Chief Inspector Parker. "You know Miss Farquson. Is she the kind of lady to protect a dead friend from scandal?"

Parker mulled it over and finally said slowly, "She's a fine person. Yes . . . she is the type. After all, this Von was her brother's widow. Has a great feeling for family, Miss Farquson."

Kepesake rubbed his hands together. "You said a couple of items, Forsythe."

"The other point that puzzles me is Marcia Mather's manner when she came down that evening to get Dowling. She didn't beg him to go with her; she practically ordered him. Even Dowling remarked on her manner. He said she was like 'a pussy full of cream.' Yet, according to his statement, a few moments afterwards Marcia was begging for a larger part."

"Something fishy there, too," Kepesake agreed. "I'd better have another word with Dowling. Beau, you get on to this Veronica Farquson lead. Find out exactly where she was twelve years ago on May the twelfth. Where are you going, Forsythe?"

"Anywhere but here." Forsythe coughed. "Much more of this smoke and my lungs will be destroyed. Why don't you switch to a pipe?"

Brummell winked at the barrister. "Now where would the chief find a jade pipe?"

Kepesake paid no attention to his sergeant. "Anything more, Forsythe?"

"You've drained me dry," the barrister said.

"If anything else occurs to you I'll be at the—"

"Unicorn in Bury-Sutton," Forsythe said and thankfully closed the door behind him.

He headed across the entrance hall and pulled the door open. Stepping out on the portico he inhaled deeply. The air was fresh, a bit too fresh. The wind, driving icy rain ahead of it, beat against the front of the house. Regretfully, he stepped back into the hall. He looked around, shrugged his shoulders, and mounted the staircase. At least the rotten weather had doubtless driven the media and gawkers away from the gates. He pitied the constables still on duty there. Perhaps they'd sought shelter in the remains of the gatehouse. When he reached the landing he found Miss Sanderson, her arms piled high with linen, scurrying along the hall. "How about lending a hand?" she called.

"I know less about housework than you do."

"No matter, I'm desperate. These bedrooms are a shambles. Clothes thrown willy nilly and the beds must be changed. Honoria's downstairs trying to cope and—"

"All right, Sandy. Tell me what to do."

She told him, and Robert Forsythe, eminent barrister and sometime detective, found himself acting as a chambermaid. He changed linen, aired rooms, hung up clothes, and dusted bureaus. As he carried soiled sheets out of Cochrane's room he spotted his secretary pounding at a door at the far end of the hall. "I'll leave the sheets here, Mickey," she yelled. "If you don't put them on you can sleep in dirty ones." Pushing her hair off her forehead, she bellowed at Forsythe. "How are you coming?"

"I'm thinking of complaining to my union. That is, if housemaids have a union." She came closer and he lowered his voice. "Having problems with Mickey Darling?"

135

"He flatly refuses to let me in. Seems to think I'm going to put a poisonous snake in his bed." She added darkly, "If I could locate one I might do it."

"As a matter of interest, how does he make it back and forth to the bathroom?"

"The Mickeys of this world have always landed soft, Robby. There's not only a study connected to the colonel's bedroom but also a large cupboard converted into a lavatory."

"And the rest of us have to line up for the main one."

"Speaking of bathrooms, have you cleaned it up yet?"

"No, and I'm not about to."

For a moment it seemed Miss Sanderson would let out another bellow. But she reconsidered. "You do look fagged so I'll let you off. You've done a smashing job and if you ever need a recommendation for domestic work come to me. Did you have lunch?"

"No, and I'm not coming down for tea. I'm going to try to get a couple of hours of sleep."

He settled eagerly on his freshly made bed, pulled a blanket over himself, and closed his eyes. A soft tap sounded on his door and he groaned and called, "Come in, Sandy."

It was Giles's voice that said, "Settling down for a nap, eh?"

"Trying to," Forsythe told him ungraciously.

Giles was balancing a bottle and two stacked glasses. He put them on the bureau and proceeded to pour. "Not for me," Forsythe said. "I've had rather too much brandy lately."

"So have I, so I had the good sergeant smuggle in some double malt. Not a bad chap but Brummell has a touch of gallows humor. Advised me not to leave the bottle standing around where someone could drop cyanide into it." Handing the other man a glass, the writer sank down onto the easy chair.

136

Forsythe lifted the glass and inhaled. After a moment he realized with grim amusement that he was trying to distinguish the telltale scent of bitter almond from the odor of whiskey. He glanced across at Giles and found the man's nostrils quivering. "Well," Giles said defensively, "I suppose it's only natural." Their eyes met and both men laughed. "Cheers, Robert. By the by, this drink is in the nature of a consolation prize. Your sleuth has come up empty-handed."

"Wouldn't Mel cooperate?"

"He tried. Said he was in London and attended Meg's funeral. He did remember at the time Erika was in Los Angeles working. He couldn't remember Von being at the service, so he figures she was probably hovering over her daughter as usual. Want me to have a try at Sam?"

"Not necessary. Chief Inspector Kepesake is taking it in hand." Forsythe drained his glass, looking crossly at his companion, hoping Giles would drink up and leave. But the writer was settling himself comfortably.

"If it doesn't conflict with your vow of secrecy I was wondering if you could tell me which one is the dummy and which the ventriloquist."

Forsythe lifted his head. "I don't follow you."

"Kepesake and Brummell. Which one is the brains of that outfit?"

"Adam Kepesake does happen to be the chief inspector."

"A typical lawyer's answer." In a gesture of wicked mimicry Giles made a waving motion and the barrister could almost see a jade holder in the writer's long fingers. He also mimicked Kepesake's voice perfectly. "Tell him, Beau," he said airily.

Forsythe smiled. "I see you've tumbled. Kepesake is fairly competent but Brummell is far out in front with ability."

"Then why is Brummell sergeant?"

"It's still rather common to find the man with the birth, the breeding, the education, receiving the promotions."

"And poor Beau looks like he tumbled out of a haystack. Think he resents Kepesake?"

"I've the impression he's rather fond of his chief. He certainly does his best to make Kepesake look good. You know, Giles, you're a man of many parts. That imitation of the chief inspector was good. Sure you're not an actor?"

Pulling his rangy frame up, Giles gathered up the glasses and the bottle. "The Lord forbid! But when you hang around with actors long enough some of it is bound to rub off. I'll leave you to your nap. See you at dinner. Wonder if Honoria will be able to rout Mickey out."

"I doubt it," Forsythe said and rolled over, burying his face in the pillow.

When he stepped from his room freshly shaved and impeccably dressed he found he'd underestimated his hostess's power of persuasion. A short procession was making its way toward the staircase. In the lead was his secretary and Erika Von Farr. Forsythe didn't spare a glance for Miss Sanderson but feasted his eyes on the actress. Erika certainly didn't look like a ghost. She was a vision in jade silk with gold bangles on her wrists and more gold glinting from her ears. Behind them Giles, wearing a dumbfounded expression, was walking at Michael Dowling's side.

"What an ordeal this has been," Dowling told Forsythe with no preliminaries. "How I've suffered."

He showed no signs of suffering. His skin was glowing with health and his curls were glossy. He was dressed nattily in a yellow cashmere sweater and white duck pants. Forsythe lifted his brows at Giles and the younger man grinned back. "Found out how Honoria did it. Hit our boy where it hurts. Told Mickey she was cutting off his kitchen privileges. Said he could starve if he didn't come down for dinner."

"I'd got sick of that room anyway," Dowling told them. "And the food! For two days I've existed on tinned soup and sandwiches."

"Think the danger is over, old boy?" Giles asked.

"Erika tells me the chief inspector did leave a man here. He let me think there wouldn't be a policeman within miles of the house. We didn't hit it off, you know. Kepesake's so thin-skinned. I called him 'my man' a couple of times and he fairly flew at me. But I stood right up to him. Told him as a policeman he was a public servant and—"

"Adam Kepesake is the son of a baronet," Forsythe said quietly.

"I don't care if his father's an earl. He's only a dumb cop."

Giles shook a baffled head. "By any chance did you mention that as a taxpayer you are paying his salary?"

"I might have mentioned it. Why?"

"Mickey, promise if you ever decide to change professions you won't go into the diplomatic corps."

"I've no intention of being anything but an actor. I'll tell you why."

All the way down the stairs, Dowling told them why. When they entered the dining room he greeted Honoria and the other two men casually and headed directly to his chair. Forsythe took a place opposite the actor and watched him covertly. Under other circumstances it might have been funny. With hawklike intensity, Dowling followed the old butler's every move. When his plate was set before him he leaned back and waited until the other diners had sampled the course before falling on his ravenously. Waiting for someone to sprawl on the floor and start having a fit, Forsythe decided. Michael Dowling inspired him with amused contempt. A dangerous way of thinking, he decided, so easy to throw a person off whatever the actor actually was. If this man had managed to outwit a bright bunch of lads in the Narcotics Division he must be cunning indeed.

Forsythe transferred his attention to the other dinners. Hardly a word was being exchanged. He'd thought Michael Borthwick would be jubilant at hearing about the inquest, but he proved as taciturn as Cochrane. Erika and Miss Sanderson were quiet and Mickey Darling was engrossed in his food. With some concern, Forsythe eyed their hostess. Honoria appeared withdrawn and abstracted, attending to her guests' needs in a perfunctory manner. The only spasm of conversation came as Potter shakily carved the ham.

"Where's the man Kepesake left here?" Dowling asked.

With a visible effort Honoria aroused herself from her thoughts. "Constable Jenkins is having his meal in the kitchen."

"Think I'll speak to him after dinner. See whether we can strike a bargain."

Borthwick examined his star warily. "What kind of bargain?"

"I don't imagine the rate of pay is high for a constable."

"Mickey, are you thinking of offering him money?"

Dowling shrugged. "If he'd keep an eye on me tonight I might make it worth his while."

"For God's sake!" The director clawed at his naked skull as though wishing for a thick head of hair to tear off. "The man will have you on charge for trying to bribe an officer."

Dowling looked sulky and for moments ate in silence. Then he lifted his glossy head and stared across at Forsythe. "Hey, I forgot. You're sort of a detective, aren't you? You bodyguard me until after the inquest and I'll pay handsomely."

"Robby," Miss Sanderson said icily, "is not a bodyguard."

"Keep out of this, Abigail. Well, Robert, what about it?"

An eerie chuckle from Giles Eady swung Dowling's head

in that direction. "Have you ever thought, Mickey, Robert might have been the one to slide that poison in your booze?"

"I trust Robert. We only met a few days ago."

"With you that's quite enough time to want to murder. Right, Mel?"

Honoria Farquson brought the flat of her hand down on the table with such force the plates jumped. "That's quite enough, Mr. Eady! Your attempt at humor is in the worst possible taste. Have you forgotten that Marcia died in this house two evenings ago? Your friend, my friend . . . she died an agonizing death."

Lowering his head, the writer mumbled an apology. Honoria turned her attention to Dowling. "As for you, Mickey, you've been shut in that room too long. What you need is exercise and fresh air. Directly after dinner you're going for a walk."

"It's pouring and it's cold, Aunt Honoria."

"The rain stopped an hour ago. As for being cold, bundle up well. I'm going to."

"You're going to walk with me?"

"Yes, Mickey." She smiled at him. "I'm going to bodyguard you."

Something about that smile disturbed Forsythe. He brooded about it until dinner was finished. Dowling and Honoria disappeared for a few moments and when they returned their hostess was wearing a shabby knitted coat that made her look shorter and heavier. Dowling's expensive doeskin jacket was buttoned to the throat. The others headed across the hall to the drawing room but Potter stopped Forsythe. "A telephone call for you, sir. Chief Inspector Kepesake ringing up from the village."

Kepesake said rapidly, "I know you can't say much at your end but Brummell's had a report on Erika Von Farr and her mother. At the time of Margaret Cochrane's accident they were both in Hollywood. Shoots your theory full of holes, doesn't it?"

"Looks that way."

"I rather liked it. Would have explained a lot of things. I've been wondering whether Dowling would have anything else on Miss Farr. Think about it, will you?"

"I'll do that," Forsythe told him, and with a smile added, "my man."

Kepesake gave a howl and Forsythe rang off.

In the drawing room the barrister paused to gaze down at the woman they'd been discussing. She was stretched on a divan with jade silk mounding gracefully over her thin body. Her eyes were closed and her face wiped so clean of expression that she appeared to be sleeping. As he watched, thick lashes lifted and he looked down into her eyes. Those eyes had no more expression than her face. Then a trace of animation flickered and Erika said softly, "I feel exhausted, Robert."

"Well all do," he told her and wandered over to the hearth. Taking the chair across the hearth rug from the wing chair where Cochrane appeared to be sleeping, he stretched out his bad leg and put his head back. In another wing chair the director's small form was engulfed and he was not only sleeping but gently snoring. Near Borthwick, Miss Sanderson and the writer had set up a jigsaw puzzle and had their heads bent over it. The heat from the fire was making Forsythe drowsy. His nap before dinner had merely been an uneasy doze and he felt unbelievably weary. I'll close my eyes for a few moments, he told himself. He closed his eyes, a thick dark curtain seemed to fall, and Forsythe fell with it.

CHAPTER ELEVEN

FOR MOMENTS AFTER FORSYTHE ROUSED FROM DEEP sleep he had no inkling where he was. He was conscious of being comfortable, softness under him and some woolly warmth over him, but whether he was in bed in his flat in London or in the wider bed in Sussex, he couldn't tell. Then he found his feet were resting on an object that felt like a hassock, his back braced against a chair. The Farquson drawing room, he thought, and opened his eyes.

There was little light, only that flickering from a dying fire and one shaded table lamp across the room. Enough light for him to see that except for the figure in the wing chair across the hearth rug the room was deserted. "How long have I slept?" he asked.

"Hours, Mr. Forsythe, it's well after midnight." Honoria turned her head and a log crashed down on the grate. Flames shot up, their light ruddily outlining the curve of a cheekbone, burnishing the long line of her jaw. "Abigail was intent on sending you to bed but I persuaded her to leave you where you are. We did put the hassock under your legs and an afghan over you."

"You haven't waited up on my account?"

"No, after the day I've had it's been pleasant just to sit idly and watch pictures in the flames. Do you ever do that?"

"Many times. What did you see in the flames?"

"My youth. I suppose that's what we look for. Happy times." She looked again into the rekindled fire and the reflected light reddened her pale hair, cast a rosy glow across the high bridge of her nose. "Abigail tells me your father was not only a barrister but a judge."

"As was my grandfather. Forsythes have always been drawn toward the legal profession."

"Then perhaps you will give me your opinion of justice."

"Our judicial system or in the abstract sense?"

"Both."

"Well, in the practical sense our system of justice is imperfect. I suppose one could expect little else of something created by imperfect man. It's a huge, creaking machine that sometimes spews out the guilty and lets them go free. At times, and thankfully this is rarer, it gobbles up the innocent. But on the whole . . . it does serve a useful purpose and is certainly much superior to vigilante justice."

"And the abstract?"

"The blindfolded figure of a woman holding scales?" Pushing away the hassock, he lowered his feet. "Throughout my life I've noticed rather an odd and at times satisfactory phenomenon. I'll give you one example. A number of years ago a friend of mine—a superintendent of the C.I.D.—had a case that obsessed him. Grantham was investigating a number of murders of prostitutes in the East End—"

"Similar to Jack the Ripper?"

"Along those lines. Grantham had his eye on a young man from a good family who always seemed to be turning up on the case. This man—let's call him John—had a

144

deformity, a club foot. In time John admitted to Grantham that his father had lived a wild life in his youth and at the time he—John—was conceived was suffering from a social disease. John blamed his deformity on this and had a paranoiac hatred of prostitutes.

"Grantham did everything in his power to prove John was killing the girls. He had him in to assist police inquiry a number of times; he put detectives on John's every movement; but he couldn't get proof that would stand up in court."

"John was getting away with murder—literally."

"Precisely. The duel went on between Grantham and John until the number of victims reached four. Then abstract justice intervened."

"John slipped," Honoria guessed. "Grantham got proof."

"No. He was far too wily for that. John decided to take a vacation. He went to Brighton. He was a strong swimmer but he got a cramp and in full view of crowds on the beach, he drowned. He went under screaming for help and not one person realized his plight or came to his aid."

She propped her chin on a hand. "Divine intervention, Mr. Forsythe?"

"Perhaps. Perhaps what we call fate, or sometimes justice. But I've often noticed that when our legal system can't touch a criminal something else seems to do our job."

"Tell me, if your friend Grantham had been on that beach . . . would he have tried to save John?"

"I can't answer that. I've no idea what another person would do."

"Would you have tried?"

Folding the afghan, Forsythe placed it across the hassock. "I would never interfere with fate."

He stood up and so did his hostess. She reached for a side table and he noticed a tray bearing a thermos jug, a fine china cup, a dish of biscuits. He took it up and followed her into the entrance hall. In the dim light he could see an easy chair had been moved into it and a young constable hopped up. He was a stocky young man with sandy hair. Honoria passed and wished him a pleasant good night. "Potter has left coffee and sandwiches in the morning room, Constable Jenkins. Do help yourself."

"Thank you, Miss Ferguson," Jenkins said and gave her a look of respect blended with affection. This man, Forsythe recalled, had once been in Miss Farquson's Sunday school class.

When they reached Honoria's room the door stood ajar and the terrier scampered to greet its mistress. She scooped up the dog and replaced it in the basket. In the strong light from the lamps her face was drawn, the skin grayish. "I hesitate to ask another favor, Mr. Forsythe, but will you be good enough to take Ciara down to Potty? I'm going to close my door and she is such a silly thing, she'll be quite upset."

Forsythe took the basket and looked searchingly down at her. "Is there . . . Miss Farquson, do you want to talk?"

"No. I'm talked out. Tomorrow will be soon enough."

She was holding open the door and Forsythe stepped into the hall. After the door closed he stood clutching the basket. Then he retraced his steps. Jenkins was at the foot of the stairs, gazing up. "Something amiss, sir?"

"No, constable. Would you be kind enough to take this little animal to the cook's quarters? Tell Mrs. Potter that Miss Farquson is closing her door tonight."

On his way to his room the barrister stopped outside Honoria's door and listened. As Kepesake had mentioned, the doors in this house were two-inch oak. He couldn't hear a sound. In his own room the bed, fresh sheets turned down over a down comforter, beckoned. He took off his jacket and vest, loosened his tie, and opened the wardrobe. He'd brought two robes. One, a fanciful silken affair, had been a birthday gift from his secretary, and the other was an old friend—shabby, woolen, warm. Pulling the woolen robe on, he pulled the easy chair away from the wall, opened the door a crack, and turned off the lamp. Sinking into the chair he could see dim light shining against Honoria's door. I'm being a fool, he thought, deserting a warm bed for this cold vigil. But his sense of unease would prevent him from sleeping soundly anyway. Something was amiss with Honoria Farquson. Her preoccupation during the dinner hour, that enigmatic smile she'd turned on Dowling, the recent conversation about justice . . .

Through the night hours Forsythe kept his lonely vigil. At times he would doze, then jerk up at a sound from the hall. Twice he leaped to his feet at the thud of footsteps. Both times it was Constable Jenkins, moving down the hall to the far end and then returning.

A third time the noise that disturbed him was softer, the creak of a door. This time he looked around his own door and saw Cochrane, attired in striped pajamas, padding into the bathroom. Forsythe stayed at his post until the huge man, carrying what looked like a glass of water, returned to his room.

Later, exhaustion overwhelmed the barrister and he was drifting off to sleep when a hand descended on his shoulder. He jerked awake. Potter was bending over him. "You've not been to bed, sir?"

Forsythe stretched and glanced at the window. Pale fingers of dawn showed in a crack between the curtains. "No, but I think I may crawl in for a couple of hours." He looked at the face close to his own. "Something bothering you?"

"Miss Honoria, sir. It's twenty after seven and unless she's ill she's never been in bed after seven."

"Probably sleeping in. She was worn-out last night."

"Perhaps, sir." Potter didn't sound reassured. "I think I'd better knock and see if she's unwell."

As Forsythe drew back the curtains he could hear the mutter of Potter's voice in the hall. His unease of the previous night returned and he found himself drawn to the butler's side. A door further down the hall creaked open and Miss Sanderson, her hair mussed and pulling a robe over her flannel gown, joined them. "What's up, Robby?"

"Potter's a bit concerned. Miss Farquson seems to be sleeping in."

Miss Sanderson yawned. "She could have taken something to help her sleep."

"Never!" Potter declared. "Miss Honoria doesn't like drugs. All she has is hot chocolate to relax her.".

Forsythe rubbed his bristly chin and stepped closer to the door. "I'll have a go." He rapped sharply and called, "Miss Farquson."

The butler's rheumy eyes turned pleadingly up to Forsythe. "Something is wrong, sir."

Forsythe now believed there was. He was about to send Potter in search of the constable when that worthy appeared on the landing. Forsythe explained and Jenkins took over. The strong fist of the law rang out against the oaken panel and several doors opened and heads popped out. "Back in your rooms," Jenkins ordered. "And stay there!" He tried the knob. "Locked." He turned to the barrister. "Think we'd better have that door down, sir."

"I agree. But how? No use putting our shoulders against it. When this house was built they didn't fool around. This is solid wood and the hinges are strong."

Jenkins swung on the butler. "Got a pry bar around?"

"In the pantry. I'll get it."

The old man took a couple of tottering steps and Jenkins told him, "I'll get it. Tell me its location."

He went to get it. Miss Sanderson was supporting Potter,

speaking to him in the soothing voice one uses for frightened animals and small children. Jenkins was soon back, taking the stairs two at a time. "Stand back," he ordered and positioned the tapered end between the frame and the lock. Even with the leverage of his youthful strength, it took time before the wood around the lock splintered and the door gave. He stepped into the room and then called, "Mr. Forsythe!"

The barrister took a deep breath and followed the young man. The curtains were drawn over the window but the room was brilliant with lamplight. The tray sat on the Sheraton desk but now the top of the thermos was off and the china cup was on the desk blotter. Also on the blotter was a sheet of writing paper. Jenkins was on his knees beside a huddled form near the desk. Honoria had collapsed on her face, one arm bent under her body, the other thrown above her head. The fingers of that hand had clawed at the nap of the carpet and were locked in that position. A robe of cornflower blue twisted around the still form. It was hiked up over one leg displaying an inch of pink flannelette and a shapely white calf. Without thinking he bent to twitch the robe down. Jenkins told him sharply, "Don't touch anything!" Then he raised his head and for a minute his training deserted him. There was grief in his face, the grief of a young boy who had affection for a one-time teacher. "She's cold, Mr. Forsythe. Rigid. Must have died hours ago."

Forsythe nodded, stepped over to the desk, noticed a ballpoint pen on the floor near it, and bent over the notepaper. Both men read the flowing writing. "Not suicide," Jenkins breathed in Forsythe's ear.

Forsythe bent lower and sniffed at the cup. It was half full and a scum had formed on the milk. "Murder, constable. Better get on to Chief Inspector Kepesake."

Jenkins opened the door. Miss Sanderson had her arms around the butler. Her face was frightened. Potter looked directly at Forsythe. The barrister flinched at the depths of anguish in those eyes. "Is she . . ."

"Yes," Forsythe told him gently. He didn't feel gentle. He felt wild with rage. Here was one of the few mourners for Honoria Farquson, not Erika, who had known her aunt for only a short time; not the villagers, who had known her charity for a lifetime and could still gossip about her to the media. An old couple who had never had a child and had taken a lonely little girl into their hearts had been dealt a fatal blow.

Potter put Miss Sanderson aside firmly but with dignity. He straightened his shoulders. "What can I do to help?"

Forsythe stepped out into the hall. "Go to your wife, Potter. Take care of her. A moment, constable. Sandy, did your sister leave a forwarding address with you?"

"Yes, and a number in case of emergency."

"As soon as the constable has finished with the telephone you ring through to Teresa. Don't let her put you off. Tell her she's the last of the musketeers. This is what I want you to find out."

He told her concisely. Then he said to the constable, "Stay with Miss Sanderson. When she leaves the house go with her. I'll take the responsibility."

They left, Sandy and Jenkins flanking Potter. Potter was moving more quickly than was his wont. Forsythe took a quick look down the hall at the row of blank doors and then returned to the room. Like a sentinel he stood over the body, angry eyes raking the room. He looked at the desk, at the table crowded with memorabilia, at the corner where Ciara's basket had sat.

After a time he said aloud, "Justice *will* be served. *Requiescat in pace*."

CHAPTER TWELVE

CHIEF INSPECTOR KEPESAKE AND SERGEANT BRUMMELL broke something of a record getting from the Unicorn in Bury-Sutton to the Farquson estate. They found Robert Forsythe still standing over the body. As they entered the bedroom Forsythe left his post and backed against a wall. Brummell examined the tray on the desk while his superior knelt beside the body. Kepesake got up, dusted off his knees, and scanned the letter on the desk. "Does this mean anything to you, Forsythe?"

"Yes, I've sent Miss Sanderson to find it. I told Constable Jenkins to stay with her."

"Same modus operandi as Miss Mather," Brummell said. "Only this time the cyanide was put in chocolate. I'd say in the thermos."

Swinging around, Kepesake eyed the barrister's shabby robe, his unshaven chin. "Chief Inspector Parker and the lads should be here soon. Want to take time to freshen up?"

"No, we'd better get to work. Did you leave men to patrol the grounds last night?"

"Williams and Stevenson. You want them?" Brummell asked.

"Yes, and Mrs. Potter, and Jenkins when he gets back."

Brummell's untidy head swung around toward the chief inspector. "The lab boys will be going over this room. Want to talk down in the library, chief?"

"I suppose we'd better." Kepesake stepped out of the room and beckoned Constable Summer. "Stay here until Chief Inspector Parker arrives. Then get Williams, Stevenson, and the cook and bring them to the library."

"What about the other people? They're poking their heads out and complaining."

"Tell them to remain in their rooms. I'll speak with them later."

The library had been restored to order. The books had been replaced on the shelves. Forsythe wondered if the police had done it or if it had been Honoria's capable hands. He stepped to the bookcase and saw the volumes about the Crimean War in their usual place, the Second World War to the right, Napoleonic history directly above. Honoria Farquson, he thought, putting her house in order, and he felt hot rage congealing into icy fury. Touching his arm, Brummell said with awkward gentleness, "You were fond of the lady, Mr. Forsythe?"

"She was a fine woman, warm and generous and courageous. Yes, I was fond of her." Forsythe sat down opposite Kepesake and started, without prompting, to speak. There were many interruptions. Miss Sanderson, tailed by Constable Jenkins, came into the room. She'd slipped a raincoat over her robe and it was glistening with moisture. The bottom of her robe was sodden and streaked with grass stains. She put down a black plastic bundle in front of the barrister. Using a pencil, he pushed it over to the chief inspector. "Get up and change those wet clothes," he told her. "Jenkins, you stay. We've a question to ask you."

Forsythe asked the question, the constable replied, and Kepesake told Jenkins, "Get up to the murder room. As soon as that letter is dusted for prints, bring it down here."

Shortly afterwards Williams and Stevenson entered the library. Rain dripped from their slickers over the gleaming parquet. Mrs. Potter, shepherded by Constable Summer, was the next person who answered questions. She seemed to be bearing up better than her husband had. Brummell questioned her but she pointedly looked at Forsythe as she answered. Kepesake was busily extracting an envelope from the black plastic wrapping. Without looking at his sergeant he extended a hand. Brummell searched in a sagging pocket, found a pair of tweezers, and handed them to his superior.

Forsythe got up to escort the cook from the room. At the door he placed a comforting hand on her shoulder. "It will soon be over, Mrs. Potter."

She looked up and her composure cracked. Behind it he could see his own icy rage. "It *is* over. She's dead. Nothing can bring her back."

Men came and went. The pathologist, whom Forsythe had met briefly at the time of Marcia Mather's death, spoke briskly and told them nothing they didn't already know. A technician brought down Honoria's letter and gingerly picked up the one on the black plastic. "There'll only be three sets of prints on that," Forsythe told him. "One will be Miss Mather's, another, Miss Farquson's."

"The third?"

"That will probably be on file with Central Bureau."

"Any idea of the name?"

It was Sergeant Brummell who told the technician the name. Kepesake was leaning back in his chair, lighting a cigarette, glowing with satisfaction. "Well, that certainly wraps this one up fast!"

"At a price," Forsythe said harshly. "Let's get it over with."

"You seem to be calling the shots, Forsythe. Who do you want and where?" •

"Dowling, Miss Farr, and Cochrane. In the drawing room. I couldn't care less about the rest."

"You'd better, Robby," Miss Sanderson said from the door. "Borthwick is threatening lawyers and Giles general mayhem if they aren't allowed out of their rooms."

"Jenkins, Summer," Brummell called. "Jenkins, bring Mr. Dowling, Mr. Cochrane, and Miss Farr, down to the drawing room. Summer, you bring Mr. Borthwick and Mr. Eady down to the morning room. And stay right with them, both of you. Where's Chief Inspector Parker?"

"In the victim's room, sergeant."

"Ask him to step down to the drawing room." Brummell looked at Forsythe. "Anything else?"

"Miss Sanderson comes with me."

"Very well," Kepesake said. "Do you want to handle it from here in?"

Forsythe took Miss Sanderson's arm. "Now it's your case, chief inspector. Sandy and I are only spectators."

They took spectators' seats. Forsythe sank down on a chair against the wall; Sandy nudged over a hassock and positioned herself beside his knee. She leaned against him and asked in a whisper, "What *was* in that package, Robby?"

He patted her shoulder. "You'll know soon enough."

Kepesake strode into the room followed by his sergeant. On their heels was Constable Jenkins, herding three people. Michael Dowling was as well groomed as ever and Erika wore a floor-length Chinese gown. Serpents and exotic flowers glowed in silken splendor against white satin. Her hair was loose and fell around a bewildered face. They perched on a loveseat, close together, Erika clasping one of

Dowling's hands in both of hers. Cochrane crossed the room and claimed his favorite chair near the hearth. The fireplace in which Honoria Farquson had watched pictures the night before was cold with a tumble of gray ashes. The room seemed as cold and Erika shivered. Chief Inspector Parker was the last to arrive. He turned a grim face to Kepesake and the other inspector jerked his head. Parker circled the loveseat and stood behind it, one hand resting on its back.

"Just what in hell is going on here?" Dowling demanded. "Keeping us shut in like prisoners."

Erika squeezed his hand. "Is something . . . has something happened to my aunt?"

"Your aunt is dead," Kepesake said.

"Oh my God!" Dowling looked terror-stricken. "Another attempt to murder me!"

"No, Mr. Dowling. The murderer got the intended victim." Kepesake looked at his sergeant and Brummell lounged across the room and halted a couple of feet from Cochrane. After a moment Jenkins strolled over casually and stood on Cochrane's other side.

Only then did Kepesake move. He pulled the tea table out a few inches and sat down behind it, facing Erika and Dowling. On the table he placed an envelope and a sheet of paper covered with Brummell's scrawl.

"You'd better tell us something right now," Dowling blustered. "I'm sick and tired of your high-handedness—"

"Patience, Mr. Dowling," Kepesake told him calmly. "In a short time you'll know what we do."

"I think," Erika said with the same calm, "it's time to make a charge or let us go. Our nerves, particularly Mickey's, can't take much more of this."

"I am making a charge. Mr. Dowling, I am formally charging you with the murders of Miss Marcia Mather and Miss Honoria Farquson."

The muscles in Dowling's handsome face went slack and

his mouth trembled. It was Erika who jumped up, her eyes flashing. "You're out of your mind! Someone tried to kill *Mickey*."

"Sit down, Miss Farr. You're only present on sufferance. Mr. Dowling's life was never in danger."

"I want my lawyer," Dowling muttered.

"In good time. When we reach the station house in Elleston you may call for legal aid."

Dowling's mouth firmed. "Let's see you try to prove this." He was suddenly cool, his expression calculating.

Picking up the sheet of writing paper, Kepesake cleared his throat. "This is a copy of an unfinished letter found in Miss Farquson's room. Mr. Forsythe escorted her to her room last evening and it would seem as soon as he'd left her she started to write this. It runs as follows." He started to read in an expressionless voice.

My dear Mr. Forsythe. If ever you read this you will wonder why I refused your kind offer to talk. At the moment I was so weary and heartsick I simply couldn't discuss it. But now I feel I won't rest until I put it down. I should imagine I will destroy this and speak to you and Chief Inspector Kepesake before Marcia's inquest tomorrow. Our conversation about justice made up my mind. All day I've been pondering, wondering whether to expose this evil or not. If I do someone I care for dearly will suffer, but at times one must speak out and help that divine intervention we mentioned. I shall try to be brief. When I met Marcia in London after all these years I was appalled. She had turned into rather a terrible person and bore no resemblance to the childhood friend I once loved. She told me dreadful things about Michael Dowling's past, hoping to influence me against him. At the time I didn't believe what she said.

Marcia came down to this house two days before Abigail and the other guests arrived. She was getting a cold and was most irritable. The second evening she had rather a lot to drink and first became maudlin about the wreckage of her life. This soon passed and Marcia started boasting about changing all that with something she had brought with her. She kept referring to this thing as her "treasure" and sometimes her "weapon." She said she not only would be able to rebuild her career but also recoup the financial losses she'd made on the film she produced starring Mr. Dowling. I'll admit my curiosity was stirred. I questioned her about it but she would tell me no more. Finally I told her if this was indeed a treasure she might better let me put it in the safe in the colonel's library. Marcia laughed and told me where she had it was "safer than any safe."

My other guests arrived the following morning and in the excitement I completely forgot about Marcia's words. It wasn't until after her death that I began to think about it. If she did have a weapon I decided it could have a bearing on her murder. It didn't take me long to come to the realization of where the hiding place was. I walked down to it and examined Marcia's treasure. Mr. Forsythe, I have always thought I was a gentle person, a woman of peace. But faced with that outrage I found myself not only horrified and sickened but consumed with a feeling of revenge. I replaced the treasure because I knew where it is *is* safe. Tomorrow I will lead the police to it and let justice take its course. I am sorry about Erika but—"

Kepesake looked up and said, "At that point Miss Farquson must have poured chocolate from the thermos and taken a swallow. The pen dug so sharply into the paper that

157

it tore." Kepesake fastened his eyes on Dowling. Under the tan his skin had gone a sickly green shade. Cochrane was no longer lounging back in his chair, he was leaning forward. His darting eyes were locked on the actor's face as though at long last they had found what they sought.

"Chief Inspector Kepesake," Cochrane's voice resounded like a drum beat, "what was Marcia's treasure?"

Kepesake pointed to the envelope. "This, Mr. Cochrane. Would you step over and see if you can identify the handwriting?"

Cochrane approached the table and bent over it. "Jenny's. Addressed to Marcia in Switzerland. She was there when . . . The postmark is the day of my daughter's death." His face was filled with agony. "Why didn't Marcia show me this?"

"Perhaps she was going to," Kepesake told him, "but she must have decided to hold on to it. She used it to blackmail Mr. Dowling."

"I think I deserve to read it."

"I think you do." Kepesake took a single sheet of paper from the envelope and spread it out. "Don't touch it Mr. Cochrane. It's evidence."

Cochrane didn't touch it. He read it slowly. Then he straightened and, moving incredibly fast for his size, sprang at Dowling. One arm swept Erika aside and his hands fastened on the smaller man's throat. Jenkins and Brummell were almost as fast. They landed on Cochrane's huge back. Parker leaped to their aid and they wrestled Cochrane away. Miss Sanderson turned and hid her face against Forsythe's shoulder. "Did you have to do *that*?"

He smoothed her hair. "Yes, Sandy, we did."

Jenkins, Brummell, and Parker were still restraining Cochrane and Kepesake moved in front of the man, looking up at him. "Our case against Mr. Dowling is airtight. Leave him to us. Let the law take its course."

"Sure! Let the bastard get a battery of lawyers and—"

"Mr. Cochrane, we'll have a conviction."

"And what will he get? Ten years? Maybe five? He *killed* Jenny. As surely as if he'd cut my little girl's throat, he killed her."

"Summer," Kepesake called. "Will you escort Mr. Cochrane to the morning room? Stay with him."

He waited until Cochrane lumbered out with Summer on his heels and then he returned to the table and sat down. Parker, still panting from the tussle, circled the loveseat and stood behind Dowling. Dowling was holding his throat in both hands. "Why did you let him read that letter?" he croaked.

"You do know what was in it, Mr. Dowling?"

"I know the lies the little fool told!"

"Jenny Cochrane told her godmother you were the man who secretly put her on heroin, who secretly seduced her. She adored you and when she found she was to have your child she went to you, expecting marriage. You laughed at her, told her she was a loose little slut and had no proof it *was* your child. She was sixteen. She couldn't face her father. She took an overdose. Do you deny this?"

"You're not getting me on a drug rap! Sure I screwed her. Why not? The little slut threw herself at me." He looked around for support from Erika but she got up, walked over to the wing chair where Cochrane had recently been sitting, and leaned against the back of it. Her face was as expressionless as it had been the evening before when Forsythe had watched her on the divan.

Kepesake was trying to conceal an expression of satisfaction and not managing it. "So, Mr. Dowling, we now have a good idea what happened the evening of Miss Mather's death. She confronted you with Jenny Cochrane's letter or, I imagine, a copy of it. You distracted her attention, slipped the poison in the bottle—"

"If this was the first time I knew about the letter how did I have the poison on hand?"

Kepesake rubbed his chin. "You're a clever man, Mr. Dowling, much smarter than you let on. I should imagine that's easily explained. Miss Mather must have mentioned something about it to you earlier. So, at the greenhouse that day you scooped up the cyanide just in case."

"All right, you win. I'll tell you exactly what happened."

"Is this in the nature of a confession?"

"No. A simple statement of fact. I didn't know anything about that damn letter until Marcia and I got up to my room. She gave me a copy and told me she had the original in a safe place. Marcia said unless I gave in to her demands she'd show it to Sam. You saw him! He'd have torn me apart! I didn't know whether to believe Marcia or not. She was such a conniving devil. I figured maybe she'd made the letter up herself and there was no original. You know what she wanted? The lead part in this film. God, can you imagine her as Catherine! It would have *ruined* me. She also wanted all the money she'd spent on that dog of a Trojan Wars, *plus interest!*"

"So you poisoned the whiskey?"

"Like hell I did." Dowling massaged the red marks on his throat. "To calm her down I offered her a drink. She poured some out and started to down it. Then she grabbed at her mouth, her eyes rolled up, and she fell on the floor. She was twitching all over and I figured she was having a convulsion or a heart attack. I was going to get help and then I thought maybe I should look in her room in case she *did* have the original of that letter. I ran down the hall and looked through her drawers and under the mattress. Nothing was there so I figured she *had* been bluffing. When I came out I noticed the row of glasses on a shelf in the bathroom so I picked one up, broke it on the floor inside my door, and

160

then called down the stairs. That is exactly what happened. I did *not* have any poison."

Brummell was looking at the actor as though the man was from another planet. "You left a woman dying to search her room?"

"Nothing I could do for Marcia and I had to think of my own skin. If she wasn't lying about that letter and Sam got his hands on it—you saw him, for God's sake! Erika, you don't believe this rot, do you?"

Her voice was expressionless as the oval of her face. "I don't know what to believe."

"Look, darling, it's a mass of circumstantial evidence. They haven't got a thing on me!"

Kepesake lit a cigarette. He waved the holder. "Tell him, Beau."

Brummell fished in a sagging pocket and brought out a notebook. He flipped it open. "Miss Farquson insisted at the dinner table, Mr. Dowling, that you walk with her."

"So? We took a walk. Damn cold it was too."

"What you may not have known is there were two constables patrolling the grounds. Constable Stevenson saw you and Miss Farquson come out the front door and start to pace up and down on the driveway. He kept an eye on you but didn't go close enough to hear what you were saying. Stevenson says Miss Farquson was doing most of the talking. You kept shaking your head and then you turned on her. You grabbed her by the shoulders and shook her. Miss Farquson broke loose and ran into the house. According to Constable Stevenson she acted frightened out of her wits."

"So?" Dowling said again. He ran his hand over his curls. "We took a walk and talked. It had nothing to do with murder or Marcia."

"It had everything to do with it. After Miss Farquson read Jenny Cochrane's letter she didn't know what to do. She was torn two ways. Any decent person would be sick at what that child said. Miss Farquson was a gentle lady, never had anything to do with violence before. You are her niece's fiancé. I think the lady wanted to give you a chance to tell your side."

"Bosh! We had a private conversation. Nothing to do with that letter."

"Then suppose you tell us what you talked about."

Dowling glanced at Erika, appeared undecided, and then shook his head stubbornly. "That, my man, is none of your business."

Brummell wasn't taking "my man" any better than his superior had. His face reddened. Curtly, he continued, "Constable Jenkins was on duty inside the house. He was in the entrance hall when Miss Farquson came running in. You were right behind her. Jenkins, tell Mr. Dowling what you heard."

Jenkins said stolidly, "Mr. Dowling yelled at Miss Farquson. His words were, 'If it's the last thing I do I'll get you!'"

"This is a frame-up!" Dowling said wildly.

"Do you deny you said those words?"

"I said them but . . ."

Brummell flipped over a page. "Jenkins says Miss Farquson went into the drawing room but you continued down the hall and entered the kitchen. According to Mrs. Potter's testimony you asked her to cut you a piece of the cake that had been served at dinner. Mrs. Potter went into the pantry, sliced the cake, and brought back a plate. When she entered the kitchen Mrs. Potter says you, Mr. Dowling, were bending over the stove. On that stove was Miss Farquson's chocolate, heating in an open saucepan."

"I was thinking of taking a cup to drink with the cake. Mrs. Potter ordered me away from it. She said it was for her mistress and if I wanted any I could make it myself. I

162

grabbed the cake and went up to my room. For God's sake check out that saucepan. I didn't put anything into it."

"Mrs. Potter never leaves dirty pans overnight, Mr. Dowling. She washed that pan up before she retired. She poured the chocolate into the thermos, arranged the tray, and took it to Miss Farquson in the drawing room. Miss Farquson drank some chocolate and died. What you hadn't counted on was the letter she left for Mr. Forsythe."

"Where had Marcia hidden that letter of Jenny's, sergeant?" Erika asked.

Brummell glanced at the corner where Forsythe sat silently. The barrister said, "In the secret mail drop the Three Musketeers used when they were children. Miss Sanderson rang up her sister Teresa, the third musketeer, and she told us its location. The three little girls used a hollow in an apple tree near the remains of the gatehouse."

Kepesake rose from behind the table. "And now, Mr. Dowling, I think you'd better come with us."

"I want a lawyer! I want him right now! Erika, get on to London and . . . for God's sake what's wrong with you?" Dowling had leaped to his feet and approached the girl. His hand was outstretched and she cringed away from him. "I've been framed! Can't you see that?"

"Don't touch me," she whimpered. Making a wide circle around him, she moved toward the door. On the back of the robe a serpent undulated its silken coils.

Dowling followed her and Kepesake, Brummell, and Parker were right behind. Pulling himself wearily to his feet, Forsythe stretched a hand out to Miss Sanderson. "Let's get packed and get out of here, Sandy."

She leaned against him and he led her into the hall. Her blue eyes were shining with tears. Brummell and the two chief inspectors were standing by the door. At the foot of the steps Dowling stretched an imploring arm upward.

Erika was partway up the stairs. Her back was toward them and she was clinging to the bannister.

"Erika," Dowling cried. "I swear I didn't kill anyone."

She spoke only two words. "*Jenny Cochrane*."

"Forgive me, darling. Erika, forgive me."

Forsythe had a strange sense of déjà vu. He watched Erika straighten, remove her hand from the bannister, and turn until she was in three-quarter profile. She wasn't crying but every line of her body showed grief and outrage. Her dark hair fell in a single fluid line down her back. Before she spoke, Forsythe, with terrible certainty, knew exactly what she would say.

"Forgiveness is impossible," said that unforgettable voice, silver swish of steel under black velvet, "but I promise I'll do my best to forget you."

"*Dark Decision*," Forsythe muttered. "The final scene."

"Robby," Miss Sanderson said gently, "she's a great actress."

"Yes. And that is all Erika Von Farr will ever be," Forsythe said sadly.

CHAPTER THIRTEEN

E̲LLESTON, NORMALLY A QUIET MARKET TOWN, IN THE days following Michael Dowling's arrest assumed an air of Mardi Gras. Buses, trains, cars, and motor bikes delivered streams of people. Among them were contingents of the Mickey Darling fan clubs, young women clad lightly and brandishing placards proclaiming their idol's innocence. Another band of young women, these more modestly dressed, had arrived to urge nuclear disarmament and wave their own banners urging Yankee go home. Mistaking these sentiments as ones directed against Mickey Darling, the fan club members gave battle. Trying to urge peace upon them and getting mauled in the process was a gaunt old man of tremendous height with a wispy beard and bare feet. Finally he lost patience and used his own placard indiscriminately against both sides.

From the vantage point of the window of their hotel sitting room, Miss Sanderson watched the melee. "That placard the old goat with the beard is beating with says 'Peace and Love.' Robby, that man can certainly fight. I feel rather glad Chief Inspector Parker smuggled us in here under fictitious names."

Forsythe looked up from his book. "So do I. I suppose we should also be glad Marcia Mather's cousin whipped away her body for decent Christian burial at some undisclosed location."

"Anyway the inquest is over and the verdict should put Dowling away for some time."

"We'll have to wait for the trial to see, Sandy. Cochrane was right. Dowling has a high-powered legal staff working for him."

She leaned closer to the windowpane. "The police are breaking the cat fight up. Look at that! A couple of sidewalk vendors peddling Mickey Darling souvenirs! Photos and T-shirts and pennants. I'd swear if they could they'd be selling locks of his curly hair!" She turned away in disgust. "You think the prosecution will get a conviction?"

"Certainly. But the sentence? Again I agree with Sam Cochrane. A few years. Perhaps long enough to demolish Dowling's career. Let's hope so."

"And his chance of marrying Erika Von Farr. Speaking of Erika, Robby, Parker told me that Sam, Mel, Giles, and Erika are still barricaded on the estate. Wonder what role she's playing now?"

Forsythe stared steadily down at a page. "No doubt woman betrayed, with Giles Eady dancing attendance on her."

"Do you suppose she'll marry him?"

He shrugged. "Never can tell but I don't think there'd be chance for practicing drama with a man like Giles." He looked bleakly at his secretary. "I'm tempted to fold our tent and slip quietly away."

"We can't. Honoria is being buried at Bury-Sutton tomorrow. We simply have to be there, Robby."

"Yes. But if you think that's rough out there—" he waved at the window— "wait until you see the funeral."

"People wouldn't . . . not at a funeral, Robby."

"It will be a three-ring circus."

It was worse. Rain fell steadily but that didn't dampen the air of carnival. Around the gray stone church and ancient graveyard crowds surged, restrained by a ring of sweating constables. In the church itself were only a handful of mourners but the vicar's words were inaudible amid the din of those outside. Several choral groups seemed to be competing. At one particularly loud bray of "We Shall Overcome" Miss Sanderson dug a sharp elbow into Forsythe's ribs. That was soon drowned out by "Onward Christian Soldiers." No doubt the militant peace marchers, Forsythe thought. Over all thundered the howl of the gray-haired prophet. "Repent" alternated with "Peace" and "Love."

Amid all this the mourners sat quietly. A black-veiled Erika was in the front pew supported by Giles Eady. Behind them were Sam Cochrane and Mel Borthwick. On the other side of the aisle were the old servants. Mrs. Potter, with her sweeping black dress, hadn't needed to don mourning but she had added a thatch of stiff black crepe pinned to her white topknot. Potter's frail shoulders were bowed and occasionally those shoulders shuddered with grief. Pool old devils, Forsythe mused, so little life left for them and now no earthly reason to continue it. The coffin had silver handles and was almost concealed beneath a blanket of orchids. Inappropriate for gentle Honoria, but what did it matter?

The burial service was mercifully brief and Miss Sanderson turned away to dry tears streaming down her cheeks. Her voice was muffled. "Let's make tracks, Robby."

"We have a gauntlet to run. Bear up, Sandy."

Even with the police forming a double line to the funeral cars it was indeed a gauntlet. The line was breached and a howling throng descended on them. Forsythe had a glimpse of a husky man, who looked remarkably like the pig farmer Cochrane had described, fighting his way toward Erika. In one hand he waved a scarlet A and seemed intent on pinning it to her black suit. Giles raised a fist and the pig farmer sprawled back into the crowd. Cochrane appeared to be breaking a photographer's camera and Borthwick was fending off a group of girls attired in shorts and T shirts. They disappeared from view and Forsythe found he had his own hands full. A middle-aged woman, her hat tipped over one eye, seemed intent on ripping off one of his lapels, presumably for a souvenir. Miss Sanderson had already lost a scarf and was squealing with fury.

Blue-clad help arrived. Jenkins and MacDonald drove the mob back from them and pulled them behind the barricade of police ringing the cars. The big Scot was panting and his face was almost as red as his hair. "Ever see anything as daft as this?" MacDonald growled.

Jenkins had lost his helmet and had a bruise on one cheek. "I'd rather be up against a gang of terrorists. Least we'd be able to use our sticks."

Miss Sanderson tugged at Forsythe's arm and pointed. "Oh God! Do something!" Forsythe looked. Summer and Williams had gotten the film people clear but he caught a glimpse of bobbing black crepe. "Come on!" he yelled at the constables and charged back into the fray.

Mrs. Potter was herding her husband in front of her and managing at the same time to fight a rear-guard action. She turned and pounded the bearded prophet over the head with her umbrella. But she was tiring. By the time the barrister reached her the crepe had been yanked off. MacDonald, harboring no ill will for the meat-cleaver incident, scooped the old woman up in his arms. Forsythe and Jenkins dragged Potter along. Forsythe threw out a fist and felt savage satisfaction when it connected with a fat red face under a Tyrol hat. When they got back to the cars MacDonald had already deposited Mrs. Potter's plump figure in the back of one. Jenkins swung Potter in beside her and stood back panting.

"We should," Mrs. Potter was declaring, "have brought Heathcliff. He'd have settled this lot down. Disgraceful!"

Forsythe braced his back against the open door and struggled to catch his breath. "It's the people involved, Mrs. Potter. Public figures. You must expect a display."

"Film people. Scarlet sinners!"

"Come now, my dear," Potter chided. "Miss Erika's an actress and she's been most kind."

"I suppose so. Give us a cottage in Bury-Sutton, Mr. Forsythe, and says she'll see to us."

I wonder, Forsythe thought, how Erika likes playing the role of Lady Bountiful. Aloud he asked, "Has she any plans for the estate?"

"Don't know and don't rightly care," the cook snapped.

"What my wife is trying to say is that with Miss Honoria gone it really makes no difference to us."

Whatever defenses Mrs. Potter had erected against emotion broke. She broke into a storm of weeping. Wordlessly she held out her hand and her husband, making soothing sounds, touched the crisp white points protruding from the breast pocket of his suit coat. He pulled out a handkerchief, shook out its immaculate square, and tenderly put it into his wife's hand. Forsythe stood, his back to the crowd, and watched these moves. Then the howls behind him seemed to fade and so did the Potters.

Robert Forsythe had a marvelous memory. In argument with friends he always insisted that the human memory is more reliable than any tape, than any computer. Tapes and computers, he was wont to say, can only transmit voices and data. The human memory is capable of playing back entire scenes at will, not only with voices and intonations, but with body language.

Now that memory clicked into place and the result caused him to sag against the car door. A hand on his arm jerked him back to the roar of the sightseers, the hoarse shouts of policemen, the faces of the Potters turned up to him. "Robby," Miss Sanderson scolded, "you're soaked. We can't do any more here. Let's go."

He mumbled goodbyes to the cook and butler and allowed Miss Sanderson to guide him to the Rover. She slid behind the wheel. "I'd better drive, Sandy," he told her. "At least until we get clear of these maniacs."

"The only way to handle maniacs is to act like one."

She proceeded to demonstrate her point. A mob of scantily clad girls lunged out in front of the Rover, waving arms and placards. Instead of hitting the brake Miss Sanderson set her jaw and brought her foot down on the gas. The girls scattered pell-mell, firm little bottoms joggling, high voices shrieking. "That," Miss Sanderson said smugly, "is how you do it."

Forsythe not only snapped on his seat belt but clung to the dashboard. It wasn't until they were clear of Elleston that he relaxed and put his head back against the seat. He was conscious of his rain-soaked coat, a dull pain in his bad knee, a soreness in his right hand. He lifted his hand and discovered the knuckles were discolored. He wondered what the fat face under the Tyrol hat looked like.

Miss Sanderson slackened speed and spared a glance in his direction. "You look as though someone bopped you over the skull, Robby."

"Someone should." He closed his eyes. "Sandy, you're looking at the world's worst ass."

"What are you raving about?"

170

"I'm a blind fool. I've been led right up the garden path."

"Look, old boy, that scene back there was harrowing. But give you a few days with your trout stream and the MacDougal and—"

"I'm not going to Scotland. I'm going to pursue a ghost so far in the past it will be a miracle if I catch it. Sandy, *don't* ask any questions—just answer one. If I don't make it back to work on time will you hold down the fort?"

"Don't I always?" She laughed and said, "Whatever you're up to—break a leg. That's show biz talk and means—"

"—good luck. Sandy, please, no more show biz. I've had quite enough."

"I," she said grandly, "will never have enough."

CHAPTER FOURTEEN

ONCE MISS SANDERSON WAS BACK IN LONDON SHE found she too had had enough of show biz for the time. After two days in her cozy flat with Aggie alternately coddling her and scolding her she sallied forth to find some enjoyment in the remaining days of her vacation. She visited with a school friend in Oxford, accepted invitations for lunches and dinners, gave a small dinner for intimates, but flatly refused three invitations for the cinema, one for theater, and another for the opera.

When she went back to work she found, as she always did after an absence, the cluttered rooms in the centuries-old building a trial. Why, she wondered, didn't they take chambers in one of the spacious new office buildings mushrooming all over the city? Tradition, Robby had said, but tradition came with smoky hearths and dripping faucets and rooms not large enough to swing a cat in.

The stolid Vincent greeted her with restrained enthusiasm and young Peters made no effort to conceal his relief. She regarded Peters with little affection and some trepidation. He was a brilliant young chap but nervous. Did he have the nervous system and the stamina required for his chosen profession?

"Trouble?" she asked.

"None," Vincent told her, "until yesterday."

"We don't know what to do!" Peters was actually wringing his hands. "When will Mr. Forsythe be back?"

"I'm not certain. Tell me about it."

Peters told her about it. "We have to have an answer for the man's solicitor. And this case . . . it's insane! I've made up a preliminary folder. Would you like to go over it?"

"Did you ring up Eugene Emory?"

"Not as yet. We thought Mr. Forsythe would be back today."

She patted his thin shoulder. "Give me the solicitor's number and I'll handle it, Peters."

She escaped from the boy and opened the door to her cubicle. Pushing the visitor's chair out of the way, she reached her desk. The walls looked even more splotched then usual. Was that a water stain? They really must find other chambers. Pushing the solicitor's number to one side she rang through to Emory.

"Gene," she said, "have you heard about the case involving Sir Amyas Dancer?"

He chuckled. "It's nearly wiped the Farquson murders off the London front pages. Weird! But the Dancers have always been a rum lot and this Amyas seems the oddest of the lot. Have you been approached?"

"According to Nervy Nellie, yesterday. Any idea what line I should take."

"Where's Robert?"

"Anyone's guess."

"Poor Miss Sanderson. Holding young Peter's trembling hand. My advice is to stall Dancer's solicitor. Let Robert make the decision. I wouldn't touch the case but it might be

173

something he'd take on. The boy has a taste for murder impossible, you know."

Taking Emory's advice she rang through to the solicitor and firmly put him off a couple of days. As she replaced the receiver she silently begged, Get back, Robby, the defense of your fort is weakening.

He didn't return the next day and by the third she was becoming worried. Could he have had an accident, she wondered; could he be in a hospital somewhere suffering from amnesia? Miss Sanderson didn't share her worry. By the evening of that third day Vincent had become infected with Peter's nerves and the rest of the staff was reacting. Miss Sanderson sent them all home early, shooing the last clerk out of the office and locking the reception door. She stopped at a stenographer's desk to stub a smoldering cigarette. That's all we need in this firetrap, she thought, and went back to her desk to deal with a mound of paperwork.

After a time she thought of going home but something held her back. Maybe, she thought, my wandering boy will turn up. Eventually her patience was rewarded. A key grated in the lock and she jumped up from her desk, tripped over the visitor's chair, and lunged into the reception area just as Forsythe was putting his pigskin case down. "Robby! Where in the devil have you been?"

"Simmer down, Sandy. What's wrong?"

"Everything. New case. File on your desk. Peters has been having hysterics and it's like the measles. The whole staff out of kilter. Robby, we simply must find other chambers. This place is driving me bonkers—"

He put a calming hand on her shoulder. "We'd better both have a drink. Break out the bottle."

"Drained the last into young Peters before I sent him home."

"Well, make it coffee. Bring it into my office."

Forsythe's office was not large but in contrast to his secretary's cubicle it seemed spacious. He was sitting behind his desk. The Dancer file had been pushed to one side. Setting the cup at his elbow Miss Sanderson took a good look at him. He was wearing a lightweight suit and had a deep tan. "You're looking fit. Where have you been?"

"On the Continent, soaking up the sun."

She took an armchair and stretched her long legs. "Soaking up the sun while I've been going bonkers. I hope you found your ghost."

"I did. Took a little doing but when I opened the cupboard it came tumbling out."

"Skeletons, Robby, that's what tumbles out of cupboards. Tell me your ghost story."

"In time. Now I'd like to hear about Dowling. Have they set trial date yet?"

Her eyes widened. "Haven't you been reading the papers?"

"I kept right away from television, radio, and papers. Why?"

"There won't be a trial. Dowling's dead. Cochrane shot him, Robby!"

He'd slumped in his chair, both hands over his face. His elbow caught the cup and Miss Sanderson rescued it in the nick of time. "Better tell me," he muttered.

She told him. When Michael Dowling had been moved from Elleston to London the police hadn't expected any real trouble. Mobs of people were swarming around but there were also mobs of police on crowd control. This time they'd used dogs and the crowd was held well back from the cars. When Dowling was helped out of the lead car, Cochrane loomed over a constable in front of him, leveled a revolver, and shot the actor twice. "Then Sam turned the gun on himself, Robby. Stuck it into his mouth and blew half his head off. Dowling died two hours later. There was a note in Sam's pocket. He said justice wouldn't be served by the light sentence his daughter's killer would get. Sam said he'd lived only to find the man and he was glad to die. He said from the moment he read Jenny's letter Michael Dowling was a dead man."

"Michael Dowling was a dead man from the moment he interfered with Jenny Cochrane. Sooner or later, Sam Cochrane would have caught up with him."

"I think Sam was only working on that film to stay close to Dowling. Robby, I don't think Sam was doing it for Erika. But what's wrong with you? I know it's a shock but if anyone deserved it Dowling did. He killed Marcia and Honoria."

His hands fell away from his face. The color had drained from his skin and the tan looked muddy. "Brace yourself, Sandy. Dowling did *not* kill Marcia or Honoria."

"Robby, you've had too much sun. As Adam Kepesake said, the case against Dowling was airtight."

"The frame was airtight. Dowling was suppose to die. First the murderer tried to poison him and when that failed decided to let the law handle him."

"This murderer . . . is he running around loose?"

"No. Now, be quiet, Sandy, and listen. You're not going to like this any more than I do but you must know. After you understand I'm going to leave it to you to pronounce sentence—"

"You mean to tell the police?"

"Or not to." Forsythe templed his fingers. "We both have excellent memories. If anything, yours is better than mine. Cast your mind back—"

"One moment. Something tipped you the day of Honoria's funeral. I think I should know what."

"A very simple act. Potter took a handkerchief from his breast pocket, shook it out, handed it to his wife. That triggered my own memory. Now, back to the evening I arrived at the Farquson house. Dinner time. Candles and dim light. What was Michael Dowling wearing at dinner?''

"How would I know? So much has happened. All right, don't push.'' Miss Sanderson's thumbnail drummed against her front teeth. "Blue . . . blue jeans, a lighter shirt . . . a scarf at his throat . . . lashings of gold jewelry.''

"The breast pocket of his shirt?''

"Something blue to match his outfit. Darker . . . a handkerchief.''

"We went from the table to the drawing room in a group. Dowling insisted Honoria go out with him for a turn on the grounds. They returned. Dowling announced his forthcoming marriage. Erika broke into tears. Take it from there, Sandy.''

"She put her hand out and Dowling didn't . . . Robby! He had no handkerchief.''

"Then what?''

"Giles—no; first Dowling asked Honoria for hers. She put her hand in the pocket of her cardigan and paper crinkled. Honoria laughed and said all she had was a shopping list. Then Giles—''

"We have all we need. It wasn't a handkerchief in his pocket, Sandy, it was a slip of paper.'' He flipped back the front of his jacket and showed her blue points sticking out of his shirt pocket. "Exactly like this one. When Honoria and Dowling returned to the drawing room she had changed her attitude towards him, was busily welcoming him into the family.''

"He blackmailed her,'' Miss Sanderson said. "In exchange for her promise about the estate he gave her that piece of paper.'' She held out an imperious hand. "Give it to me!''

"Patience. Dowling blackmailed our hostess. Now, your memory again. Next morning. Picnic planned but rain teeming down. Morning room. You arrived for breakfast before I did. What was Honoria doing?"

"Looking out of the window. She was rather sad and upset. Her picnic plans had been ruined."

"Honoria wasn't sad because of the picnic. She was sickened and despairing. The evening before, Erika's lover had blackmailed her into consenting to his marriage, among other things. At that point Honoria remembered Marcia's treasure. She didn't read Jenny Cochrane's letter *after* Marcia's death; she read it that morning when she took the walk in the rain."

"Mrs. Potter scolded Honoria about that walk. Said she'd been out in the rain before the sun was up."

"Then Honoria Farquson realized fully what Dowling was. He would have ruined Erika. Honoria had lived a life of quiet desperation; she wasn't going to let Erika's life be destroyed. She maneuvered the entire group to the greenhouse, took the cyanide, and when we returned put some of it in Dowling's whiskey."

"When Marcia died in his stead Honoria was shattered, Robby, simply shattered!" The secretary's pale eyes locked with Forsythe's. "How could she have fooled us? Robby, Honoria was such a *simple* woman."

"A natural actress, Sandy, one of the best. And she had no instinct towards murder. She did what she thought she must but afterwards . . . her childhood friend had died agonizingly. Honoria still had the rest of the cyanide but she couldn't bring herself to use it on Dowling. So, she changed course and decided to have him indicted on two counts of murder. To do this she set all of us as witnesses. The constable on the grounds, Jenkins in the hall, Mrs. Potter in the kitchen. And me. Particularly me. Sandy, that simple lady of yours played me like a trout going after live bait. That hint in her letter . . . she knew I'd follow it up and find the musketeers' mail drop. And I went for it. As though

178

Honoria were pulling me about like a puppet, I helped frame Michael Dowling for murders he didn't commit."

"Incredible! What courage she had! She put the cyanide in her thermos, probably burned its container on her hearth, wrote the letter, and drank the chocolate. Robby, I don't think she wanted to live, not after Marcia . . ."

"Nor do I. Any questions?"

"Two. How did she make Dowling so angry that night on the driveway that he laid hands on her and shouted threats?" She hesitated and then said, "Oh!"

"I can see you've tumbled. I imagine Honoria simply told Dowling she'd changed her mind and was breaking her promise. The estate would never be his. Dowling saw red. He was already counting his profit. Your other question?"

"Motive. I told you I thought Honoria was capable of crime but the motive wasn't strong enough. Robby, I'd swear she didn't even like her niece."

He flipped open his jacket and handed her the folded sheet of dark blue notepaper. "I've been in Italy, in a village in the Apennines called Santa Vittoria. As Dowling mentioned, he was there last year. He didn't spend any time looking for souvenirs. Instead he visited a doctor. Salvatore Valenti is very old now but his memory is clear. He remembered Michael Dowling and he clearly remembered the young English girls he'd taken in thirty years ago. I think the good doctor was half in love with Honoria Farquson. He called her a Viking princess. He also says he was hoping her baby would look like her. But instead of having fair hair and blue eyes her child was dark. Doctor Valenti didn't care as much for Von Farquson."

Miss Sanderson read the crabbed writing. "Not Honoria's niece. Her daughter!"

"Dowling was a cunning chap. He carefully filed this fact away just in case it might be useful to him later. When he realized there was money to be made on Honoria's property

179

he used it. Dowling had no honor but he realized that as Chief Inspector Parker said, Honoria's word was 'inviolate.' So . . . Honoria got Doctor Valenti's letter and Dowling got her promise."

Miss Sanderson laid the blue paper on the desk as though it were somehow fragile. "That's why the colonel consented to Honoria and her sister-in-law going to the Continent. He sent them away so that the baby could be born and his precious family name not be sullied. They must have switched passports and Erika was registered as Mrs. Charles Farquson's child. But this was Honoria's dream—to have children. Why didn't she take the child and run for it?"

"We can only surmise. Knowing Honoria I imagine her father extracted a promise she would return. Also knowing Honoria she couldn't stand the stigma of illegitimacy to be attached to her daughter. Also, knowing your ogre, I imagine the colonel would have allowed her to bring the baby home as her nephew if it had been a boy. It was a girl and he didn't want it. He forced Honoria to let Von Farquson take the child to the States. Remember Butterscotch, Sandy?"

"He punished by taking away a love object," Miss Sanderson said wrathfully. "Honoria loved her daughter, and he made her give up the child. I hope he's burning in hell!"

"You and Mrs. Potter. If there is any afterlife I imagine that's where he is. And amen to it."

Miss Sanderson was tapping her teeth again. "I can make a guess about Erika's father."

"I should have tumbled to that sooner. Honoria let it slip the first night I carried her tray up for her. I was examining her table of memorabilia and—"

"And thinking of nothing but Erika Von Farr."

"Yes," he said ruefully. "But Honoria said that Erika was 'so much like her father.' She covered by saying 'not in

180

looks, but in nature.' Charles Farquson was vacillating and not brainy. But Erik Larsen had, as Honoria told us, 'passion, depth, courage.' Erik Larsen was Erika's father.''

"A country mouse thrown into Bohemia," Miss Sanderson mused. "Eighteen years old and in a tiny flat with a glamorous young man. If Erik hadn't died, maybe they might have married."

"Perhaps."

"And three people are dead because of Honoria's mother love."

"More of a mother guilt. When Erika and her mother met after all those years I believe Honoria knew what her daughter had become. Sam Cochrane called Erika lopsided; Borthwick said she's a series of roles with a core of emptiness. And Honoria was the one who handed her baby over to an ambitious, driving woman. All Erika had is her acting career, and her mother did her best to protect that career. Now, your honor, the verdict."

She glanced down at the slip of blue paper. "You think Doctor Valenti's statement and the other points you've made might be enough to clear Dowling's name?"

"Possibly."

"And in doing so we'd brand Honoria a murderer?"

"Yes."

"Take me out to dinner, Robby. Ply me with that double you owe me and several others and when I'm properly befuddled I'll hand down my decision."

"Not good enough. Now, Sandy."

Her eyes searched his face. "There's no way you could have kept Sam Cochrane from killing Dowling."

"The verdict."

"Michael Dowling versus Honoria Farquson. Dowling . . . selling drugs . . . corrupting a mere child . . . driving a woman to suicide. Honoria . . . living her life in a hell devised by the colonel . . . honorable . . .

181

dying to keep her daughter, who certainly isn't worth it, from ruin. No contest."

Miss Sanderson stood, reached for the blue paper, shredded it. She threw the pieces in the air and they fluttered down like blue confetti. A few scraps caught in Forsythe's hair. "Justice *has* been served. May you rest in peace, Honoria Farquson."

ABOUT THE AUTHOR

E. X. Giroux lives in Surrey, British Columbia. She is also the author of A DEATH FOR ADONIS.